"I'm a liberated woman."

Leonie spoke firmly. "I don't have my mind set on home and husband and children."

"But you might consider them?" Charlie was leaning forward, and a fragment of a smile played around his lips.

Leonie fumbled. "Well, if something special came along, I might consider it."

"I'm not sure myself," Charlie said. "I've tried it once before. To tell the truth, marriage isn't all it's chalked up to be."

D0801955

Emma Goldrick describes herself as a grandmother first and an author second. She was born and raised in Puerto Rico, where she met her husband, a career military man from Massachusetts. His postings took them all over the world, which often led to mishaps—such as the Christmas they arrived in Germany before their furniture. Emma uses the places she's been as backgrounds for her books, but just in case she runs short of settings, this prolific author and her husband are always making new travel plans.

Books by Emma Goldrick

HARLEQUIN ROMANCE
3134—MISSISSIPPI MISS
3164—A TOUCH OF FORGIVENESS
3188—DOUBLY DELICIOUS
3303—BABY MAKES THREE
3335—THE BALLEYMORE BRIDE

HARLEQUIN PRESENTS PLUS
1576—THE WIDOW'S MITE
1608—SUMMER STORMS

HARLEQUIN PRESENTS
1465—SILENCE SPEAKS FOR LOVE
1488—SMUGGLER'S LOVE
1545—SPIRIT OF LOVE
1681—THE UNMARRIED BRIDE

Don't miss any of our special offers. Write to us at the following address for information on our newest releases.

Harlequin Reader Service
U.S.: 3010 Walden Ave., P.O. Box 1325, Buffalo, NY 14269
Canadian: P.O. Box 609, Fort Erie, Ont. L2A 5X3

LEONIE'S LUCK
Emma Goldrick

Harlequin Books

TORONTO • NEW YORK • LONDON
AMSTERDAM • PARIS • SYDNEY • HAMBURG
STOCKHOLM • ATHENS • TOKYO • MILAN
MADRID • WARSAW • BUDAPEST • AUCKLAND

If you purchased this book without a cover you should be aware that this book is stolen property. It was reported as "unsold and destroyed" to the publisher, and neither the author nor the publisher has received any payment for this "stripped book."

This novel is dedicated to Bob,
who keeps a sharp eye on all the rest of us—
whenever he can find his glasses

ISBN 0-373-03351-6

LEONIE'S LUCK

Copyright © 1994 by Emma Goldrick.

First North American Publication 1995.

All rights reserved. Except for use in any review, the reproduction or utilization of this work in whole or in part in any form by any electronic, mechanical or other means, now known or hereafter invented, including xerography, photocopying and recording, or in any information storage or retrieval system, is forbidden without the written permission of the publisher, Harlequin Enterprises Limited, 225 Duncan Mill Road, Don Mills, Ontario, Canada M3B 3K9.

All characters in this book have no existence outside the imagination of the author and have no relation whatsoever to anyone bearing the same name or names. They are not even distantly inspired by any individual known or unknown to the author, and all incidents are pure invention.

This edition published by arrangement with Harlequin Enterprises B.V.

® and TM are trademarks of the publisher. Trademarks indicated with ® are registered in the United States Patent and Trademark Office, the Canadian Trade Marks Office and in other countries.

Printed in U.S.A.

CHAPTER ONE

LEONIE MARSHAL was a sturdy girl of twenty-seven summers. Woman, rather. At five feet nine her mass of lush brown hair curved around her neck and down to the middle of her back. Ordinarily she braided it to keep it out of the way. For some reason she could never bring herself to have it cut. The mass of hair outlined a heart-shaped face—with a dimple on each cheek, mind you, and a double handful of freckles spread across the bridge of her nose.

Her figure made men turn around to look after she passed. Her blue eyes matched her sunny disposition. But without her glasses Leonie could hardly tell near from not so near, and she hated to wear her horn-rims in public. It was not that she was blind. Not by any means. It was just that things were vaguely obscure, out of focus, as if they had no edges. She had tried contact lenses, but to no avail. So it was not unusual to discover that she had left her glasses somewhere in the car, as she had today. All of which was a distinct disadvantage when she pushed her way through the swinging doors of Fairview's only supermarket on Friday afternoon.

'Why, Leonie,' one of the vague shadows said as she pulled a cart out of the rack.

'Er—yes?' Leonie mumbled as she struggled in her mind to identify the voice. 'Oh, Mrs Simpson——'

'Done it again?' her neighbour laughed as she wheeled her car away down the fruit and vegetable line.

So everyone knows, Leonie lectured herself for the hundredth time. It's no big secret. All you do is make

5

yourself look stupid, kid. Brighten up. The first thing you know you'll walk into some catastrophe, all because you won't wear your glasses! And to keep track of them all you need to do is buy one of those cords that let you wear the darn things around your neck. Right? Right! Any child of ten could do it.

For the hundred-and-first time she moved her trolley over close to the edge of the vegetable bins and began her weekly shopping, mostly by the touch-and-squint-and-feel system.

By dint of aggressive trolley-pushing and nose-to-label reading she had weighed down the four-wheeled trolley in a short time. Those who knew her dodged out of the way; those who didn't had the tendency to mutter certain nasty words under their breath as Leonie swept by. Leonie closed her ears, sighed for her reputation and charged along.

After all, she reminded herself, she had only a limited amount of time before she had to get back to the play-school. The school was open late on Friday because her two part-time assistants were available, and Friday afternoon was the time when the fewest other customers were in the supermarket. It was a case of trading time for space, neither of which she really had much to spare.

It was not until she came down aisle six, canned goods, that Leonie ran into trouble. She was wheeling away at a good clip when one of the vague shadows in front of her stopped unexpectedly, blossomed out into a large fixed pile of humanity, some part of which fell to the floor.

It was the sort of problem Leonie had not often faced before. Her mind was still wrestling with her financial problems at the school; there was a baby crying some-where in front of her. Without thinking Leonie flexed her arm muscles and steered her trolley hard left to the other side of the aisle. It was no real problem. A girl who handled milk cans every morning at six o'clock when the truck from the milk-collective came around had enough muscles developed to shift a dozen trolleys. There seemed to be something on the floor in front of her, however. Her trolley bounced over it.

Charlie Wheeler was doing his best, but it wasn't enough. The local store manager had half a dozen explanations why the tomatoes on aisle four were partially spoiled. Charlie took a deep breath. It was enough to bring the manager to an abrupt halt.

'I don't really want a lot of excuses,' Charlie said. His voice was threateningly deep, as befitting a man who stood six feet four. The fact that he was worn to a magnificent splinter had nothing to do with anything. He had been lucky to survive the car crash. A month in the hospital and five more in rehabilitation had devoured the pounds.

And in the interim his wife had deserted him, his father had died, and the chain of Wheeler supermarkets had dwindled away to this one disreputable market.

'I mean to restore this store,' he told the manager, and then snorted at his own choice of words. 'And if you can't even get the tomatoes unspoiled to the racks, then——'

The threat floated heavily on the air between them. The girl at the check-out counter was almost crawling over the register, trying to hear every word. Charlie stifled his anger and brushed his long black hair back off his forehead. His face was sharp as a bone. Two parallel scars staggered across his forehead. White, normally, but when he became angry they turned red.

This argument isn't for public display, he told himself, and then sighed. All he knew about grocery management he had learned at his grandfather's knee, and long since he had put it behind him to follow a career in computer engineering. It was senseless to chew on the man in public. He waved the store manager away.

Charlie watched him go. The man dragged his feet for a moment or two, then took a deep breath and squared his shoulders. A manager needs something like that, Charlie thought, and smiled. He wasn't aware of it but when he smiled he looked like an amiable bear. When he didn't smile he didn't look amiable.

Charlie had plans. Numberless plans, but now he was too restless to stand around thinking. He had been leaning on the corner of one of the check-out counters. Now he straightened up and tugged down the corner of his blue blazer. His legs ached. They always did by this time of day. A little walking would be good for them—and him.

There were few customers—too few for a weekend afternoon—but he smiled at all and sundry just the same. There seemed to be some confusion in aisle six. He came around the corner in his best management style. One of the shoppers had more children than groceries in her trolley. The little boy was dancing over the front wheels. The little girl was sitting high in the back, laughing away. And as he came up to them the girl giggled too much, leaned over too far, and fell out of the trolley. The child screamed. Her mother screamed. The little boy started crying——

And the shopping trolley behind them swerved over into the opposite side of the aisle, fully loaded, and ground over Charlie Wheeler's sensitive foot! Charlie's groan was more like a yelp. The foot had been mangled in his car accident, and was not exactly cured.

Charlie's grandfather had been a carpenter before he went into the grocery business. A truly religious man, he never cursed, even when he hit his thumb with a hammer. And now Charlie used the only expression his grandfather had ever permitted.

With teeth clenched, eyes raised to heaven, he roared in words that were steel, 'Jesus—Christ—is—my—saviour!'

Leonie stopped dead in her tracks. The little girl stopped yelling and turned around to stare up at him. The little boy stopped crying. The children's mother, about to make a long vocal appeal to the management, froze in position.

In the silence that followed Leonie's voice penetrated like a knife through butter. 'Don't you ever,' she said indignantly, 'yell at children!'

She moved a little closer, trying to bring him into focus. Her stomach pushed on the handle of the trolley and the vehicle rocked back and forth suggestively.

'Oh, no, you don't,' he said, shifting his foot out of danger's way. 'Once is enough! You don't get a second shot at me!'

What else she might have said went by the board. The little girl, caught between enjoyment and fear, lifted up her arms in his direction. He snatched her up off the floor and tossed her high above his head. The child giggled. The boy crowded over to Charlie's knees.

'Me?' the child said.

Any other man would be hung up on the horns of dilemma. Whether to put the girl down and favour the boy, or cut them both off. Instead, one-handed, Charlie Wheeler picked the boy up as well, and juggled them both back and forth until laughter filled the aisle.

'Thank you ever so much,' the children's mother said. In her voice was that background that made it seem she wished there were room and to spare for *her* in his arms.

Leonie's stomach turned. Nothing, she told herself, there's nothing worse than women pandering to this—person. Obviously there was a very great deal of man there. Peering closely, she began to get signals about his size—especially his height.

'You mustn't let your child ride anywhere in the cart except in the special child's seat,' Charlie said. His voice was no longer a roar, but rather a soft caress.

It was almost as if he were making love to the woman, Leonie told herself fiercely. Damned male chauvinist! I'd like to take him down a peg or two. The thought touched her funny-bone. Peg or two? Foot or two, more than likely! What do you suppose he is? The store manager? She doubted that, having done unsatisfactory business with the manager from time to time in the past. The chief bag boy? What the devil did he suppose the woman was going to do, with only one cart and two children?

He showed her. He was wearing a little whistle attached to the lapel of his jacket. It made barely a squeak. Almost immediately another young man appeared, received some instruction, procured and pushed a second trolley, and the happy family went off on its way.

'Clever,' Leonie told him. Once the family had departed she pushed her trolley over to the side of the aisle. He limped over to her. She could see the jerky motion without any trouble. All Leonie's good nature popped to the surface.

'I've really hurt you? I'm—terribly sorry.' He would never know how much that simple admission cost her. This was the decade that Leonie Marshal had sworn off men. All kinds of men. The only exception from her male-avoidance was boys under seven. No other need apply.

'It's nothing,' he said, shrugging his shoulders. Leonie couldn't see the shrug, but it seemed like something he would do.

'Nothing? I've crippled you!'

'Not exactly. Most of the damage was done by an automobile some months ago. You just added a little dollop on the top. Are you having some trouble with your eyes?'

'Me? Never!' Leonie crossed her fingers behind her back. Father Hennesy would demand ten hail Marys for that one—to pile on top of the round dozen other acts of contrition necessary from this week's work.

'Isn't that strange? I would have sworn that your eyes were—but of course not, huh? The customer is always right. My name is Wheeler. Charlie Wheeler.'

And then he puts out his hand to seal the introduction, and I don't know where the hand is, and he'll immediately think that I'm too darn proud, or hate him like the devil, she told herself.

'Leonie,' she mumbled. 'Leonie Marshal.' She didn't have to worry about where his hand was. He seized hers before she could get it more than an inch away from her side. Seized it and pumped it and then refused to let it go.

'Leonie Marshal,' he repeated. 'Nice. Every family should have one.'

He was going too fast for her. 'One what?' she asked, and felt foolish the moment the words were out of her mouth.

'One Leonie,' he answered. The chuckle was big enough to fill an ordinary room. 'One Leonie Marshal.'

Leonie felt crowded. She managed another step backwards, putting her elbows among the large canned tomatoes. The massive being in front of her came closer.

Leonie, completely at sea, held her breath. He was close enough to touch. And he was touching.

She knew what to do, of course. Any woman knew. She told herself to stand stiffly at attention, pay no mind at all to the cruising lips that brushed past her eyebrows, seeking her mouth. Unfortunately it was more than a little difficult in practice. Leonie could not remember any time in the past six years when it seemed so impossible to stand still. Her upper lip quivered as his lips touched hers. Her arms, for some strange reason, reached up to go around his neck. Her spinal cord seemed to have broken into tiny pieces, and each little segment was doing its own wild dance.

After a moment he stopped. Leonie managed, with difficulty, to catch her breath. And her good sense. 'Now why did you do that?' she demanded.

He shrugged his shoulders again. 'I don't really know. It seemed like such a good idea at the time. I enjoyed it. You didn't?'

'Enjoyment has nothing to do with it,' she said firmly. 'Propriety. One hardly expects to get kissed on aisle seven of the supermarket.'

'Aisle six.' He offered the correction and then grinned at her. He was very close, and his teeth were pearl-white. It was almost a challenge; Leonie managed to squeeze out an extra inch or two of distance between them. She squinted, and his form came more fully into view.

'Propriety?' he mused.

'Propriety,' she confirmed. 'You don't know the word?'

'Not in this context,' he said, sighing.

'Well, really.' The new voice came from behind them. 'I don't mind the kissing, but my husband will be home for supper in an hour, and I've got all his meal in this basket!'

'I believe we're blocking the aisle,' Charlie Wheeler said. He faded away from Leonie who was, at her age, nobody's fool. Leonie Marshal straightened the wheels of her trolley and dashed for the check-out counter, which, being brightly splashed with light and advertising, could be seen even by her. As the cashier totalled her purchases with lightning speed, Leonie could hear the deep, penetrating voice behind her, where Charlie Wheeler was making his excuses.

'That man back there.' Leonie prodded the cashier as she handed out her credit card.

'Oh, him? Charlie Wheeler? The big man?'

'Yes. Who is he?'

'Charlie? This is the Wheeler Supermarket. Charlie owns it.'

It was moving towards late afternoon. Late autumn afternoon in New England. With daylight saving time coming to an end the sun would set somewhere around four-thirty. A little breeze had risen, rustling the colourful leaves of the maple trees that surrounded the car park. There was a small-town freshness to the air.

The high-intensity lights came on, lighting the car park up like a football field just before a night game. Leonie made her way without much trouble, to the 1976 station wagon that waited for her.

Not an eager waiting. The car matched its years, leaning somewhat to starboard as it sat. The silencer was still attached, but had a tendency to drag on bumpy streets. All of the six streets in Fairview were bumpy. Nevertheless, station wagons made in 1976 were built somewhat on the order of Sherman tanks, and despite all the rattles and bangs they managed to hang together. Maybe it was the paint job. Leonie often thought that could be the answer. The coat of green paint was chipped in places, but otherwise hung on desperately.

She was out of breath as she wheeled her trolley up to the rear of the station wagon. Out of breath and no good reason for it. She was a hard-working girl. Up at four to milk, muck out the barn, prepare the milk to be picked up. Back to the house at seven-thirty to make breakfast for herself and Aunt Agnes. Feed the cows and turn them out to graze by eight.

Off to school at nine, downtown. In fact the only decent space for a playschool in all of Fairview. The rent was cheap, the site matched all the ordinances for private schools, and the enrolment was at a maximum—twenty-eight charming little hellions from four to six years old. There were times when Leonie wished she were half deaf instead of half blind. Or, even better, the heiress daughter of the town's richest citizen. But she had no luck in either concern.

Being a sunny woman at heart Leonie grinned at herself as she fumbled in the driver's seat for her lost glasses. And—presto!—the world became distinct. 'And I am never,' Leonie told that world, 'going to go without my glasses again! Never!'

Well, there is the high-school alumni dance in six weeks. Maybe, just once? And I'll wear that calf-length blue velvet with the deep-dip bodice, and I'll convince at least one or two that I'm not getting as old as fast as some people think! And why did he kiss me? asked a little voice inside her head.

And so thinking, she managed to get all the groceries into the van and only cracked one egg.

Charlie Wheeler took one last look around the store. Big it was. As big as it had ever been when it was the keystone of the Wheeler chain—back in the days when everything newer or cheaper had appeared under the Wheeler name in thirty-two different stores. And it'll be that again, he promised himself. Ten or more, and quickly, before Grandpa comes to the end of his chain. Before the cancer bug eats up his interest and his future. Something for Gramps now, and for Cecilia in her future.

A tiny smile lit up his face, transforming what might have looked like a sharp hatchet-face into a form of male beauty. There was a collective sigh from among the several cashiers as he went by, heading out into the car park, whistling.

The car park lights surprised him. The sun was not yet down, and the brilliant floodlights were expensive. He checked his wristwatch just to be sure. It gave him a little shock. Four-thirty already. He had one more important stop to make, and his daughter Cecilia was waiting for him at the downtown playschool. Not too patiently, he supposed. His daughter was not the patient kind.

He had parked his 1928 Packard touring car in one of the far corners of the car park. It was a completely refurbished old vehicle, worth four times as much now than when it was new. Not the sort of vehicle you park in the middle of a supermarket car park. Not by a darn sight. Which was one of the reasons he left Cecilia at the school rather than in the car.

As it happened, the car park, like the store behind him, was almost empty. But there was a car parked right in front of his. An old station wagon, with the boot opened. Somebody was trying their best to cram a few more items into it.

Being a long way from being dead, Charlie Wheeler licked his lips and stared. All that could be seen of the person at the old wagon was a well-rounded female posterior crammed into a tight pair of old grey jeans. There was a delightful wiggle or two involved. Evidently the groceries were fitting into the wagon almost as tightly as its owner fitted into the jeans. Charlie Wheeler, being a closet chauvinist, grinned his enjoyment.

But when the wagon owner popped out, Charlie wiped the grin away in micro-seconds, and did his best to appear the mature American male. 'Miss Marshal,' he called cheerily. 'Need any help.'

She stared at him through a pair of brown horn-rimmed glasses. Stared him up and down as if she had never seen him before. 'Charlie Wheeler,' he reminded her. 'Back in the store?'

'I remember,' she said, and stared some more. He was taller than she had thought. Basketball-player tall. Thin. Good lord, skinny was the appropriate word. Tooth-pick skinny. He wore a pair of grey trousers, a dark blue sweater, and a matching blazer. His hair was short and combed close. There were a pair of scars on his forehead. He stood slightly bent over, as if trying to hide his height.

'Mr Wheeler,' she repeated his name, and nodded her head. He didn't appear to have enough strength to help. 'No—no, thanks. I don't need any help.' And then a spurt of curiosity. 'Are you the store owner?'

'One of them,' he acknowledged. 'My grandfather is the major owner of the chain. Do you live in Fairview?'

'All my life.' She nodded to him again. It wasn't *quite* true. She had left the town for five years when she went to the state university. She had planned on another year or two—perhaps a Phd in child psychology—but then a multiple series of accidents at home had called her back—too late as it happened, for her mother and father had both been lost in an aircraft accident while on tour to Italy. And her new life was totally changed from what she had known and expected.

The wind came up, eddying through her hair, spreading it out in an infinitely soft, thin haze that accentuated its beauty. Her hand came up and ran through the maze in a habitual movement beyond her control. When she looked up he was grinning at her. An engaging grin. She returned it as she slammed the boot shut and walked around to the driver's door. He took it as a friendly dismissal, and offered her a half-salute, two fingers tipping at his forehead.

He walked back to the Packard, fingering the car keys in his pocket. She was a beautiful thing, no doubt about that. She wore a red ribbed sweater along with her jeans, and a tiny white scarf tied artfully around her neck. The sweater was as tight as a man could wish. And she was undoubtedly equipped with *all* the feminine structural requirements. As seen from a man's point of view, that was. Even the glasses added a little fillip to the occasion. Her blue eyes looked a little vague behind those glasses, a little perturbed, as if all the weight of all the problems in Fairview rested on her shoulders. To emphasise the possibility, her right hand quivered. Grinning again, Charlie Wheeler leaned against the front fender of his car, content to watch what else might transpire.

Leonie settled back into the driver's seat. It had been a pleasure—momentary, to be sure, but a pleasure. He was a delightful scarecrow, especially when he smiled. She would remember that smile. And that kiss was not to be ignored, either. Leonie Marshal had enjoyed more than one kiss in her lifetime. Hated some, come to think of it. Just because she was—well-built might be the word, she told herself—more males than she could enjoy had felt that an octopus grip would please her.

Of course he had kissed her. But not with a wrestling hold to strangle her into submission. All in all it had

been very—nice. Charlie Wheeler. She made a mental
note and checked his name off on the bright side of re-
membrance as she reached for the ignition key.

The engine sputtered and coughed a time or two, and
then settled down into a dulcet roar. She sighed at the
miracle. As with any careful driver, Leonie looked up
into her rear-view mirror, and then checked in her side-
mirror. He was still standing there, leaning on the front
fender of his car. He waved as he caught her eye in the
mirror. She checked again in the rear-view mirror. There
was plenty of space between her car and his.

In front of her was a small concrete bump. The car
park was full of them, to prevent speeders. She reached
for her handbrake. The manoeuvre was simple. All she
had to do was to back up a few feet, swing the wheel to
the right, and move smartly out in to the main road.
She took a second to stick her hand out of the window
and wave back to him. Her hand moved to the gear lever.
Not for Leonie the jaded life of automatic drive. Her
foot moved to the clutch. Everything was so pleasant.

Old cars sometimes made strange noises, and very
often did not respond immediately to the command to
'go'. So Leonie was not surprised that she had to jiggle
the clutch. Nor, when the heavy car began to move
backwards, was she surprised to hear a grating noise from
the rear end.

But when Charlie Wheeler screamed bloody murder,
her attention was pulled from what she was doing. She
looked over her shoulder out of the window. Charlie
was no longer leaning on the front fender. Instead he
was sprawled on the ground—and there seemed to be
something wrong with the front end of his old car. Leonie
jammed on the brakes and her station wagon came to a
grinding stop.

'Hell and damnation,' Charlie Wheeler roared as he rolled over and fought his way to his feet. Leonie opened her car door and slipped out on to the tarmac. 'What happened?'

'What happened! You ask me what happened?'

Cautiously, trying not to get too close to him, Leonie walked to the back of her car. There had been plenty of room. She knew it was so. Her eyes were a small problem, but wearing her glasses she had good vision. So how could there be any problem that *she* caused?

'What did you do?' she queried him.

'You mean today all day, or just now?' he muttered as he swiped at his dirty trousers. 'The worst thing I can think of is that I got out of bed this morning. The next worst is that I came and met you!'

'It can't be all that bad,' Leonie assured him. Her eyes wandered to the back of the station wagon—and the messy construction of wires and wheels that once had been a sturdy shopping trolley. Which she had left parked directly behind her car when she'd finished loading the groceries. And which had been pushed back into his glorious old car with all the force of her heavy wagon. The carriage had splintered, and all the chrome rods from which it was made had opened up like daggers and thrust themselves into his beautiful old radiator.

'Oh!' she sputtered. 'Oh, my goodness!' The front end of his Packard had been chopped up by the shreds of the shopping trolley. One fender had lost all the splendour of its chrome decorations. Water dripped dismally from several punctures in the radiator.

'I did that?'

'You did that, lady.' There was nothing pleasant at all in the rattle of his threatening voice.

'Well, thank goodness that yours is a very old car,' she reflected. 'It can't be worth much.'

'That is a very old *antique* car,' he corrected in a very steely voice. '*Antique.*'

Leonie gulped. Antique car. Worth——

'About sixty-five thousand dollars' worth of antique,' he said, as if he could read her mind. 'I hope to hell you've some insurance on that bomb of yours.'

'Oh, yes,' Leonie squeaked. It was true. She did have insurance. The minimum allowable in order to drive a car in Massachusetts, not anything like what the cost of repair on this—antique—would come to. Why did the legislature allow this—thing—to be on the road? She rambled desperately through her mind, trying to think of something, or someone, she could blame the whole affair on. Nothing came to mind.

'I—I'm sorry.'

He nodded, but there was nothing like forgiveness on his face. All he reminded her of was the face of the operator of the guillotine, whom she had watched more than once in re-runs of the movie *Tale of Two Cities*. Death and destruction, and Leonie was not ready for either of those. She shivered.

'Here's my card,' she said as she pawed through her little purse and pulled out her business card. 'Leonie Marshal, Fairview, Massachusetts', the card said. 'I do have to go,' she told him anxiously. 'I have a bunch of children waiting for me, and I——'

'Go,' he said. 'Go already. Only the Lord knows what might happen to me if I stand around here next to you any longer. I'll have my car repaired and then get in touch with you.'

'Yes,' she said. There was a mad itch running down her spine which told her to get out of here before something *else* happened. He didn't look like the sort of man who beat up women. But if she could get out of the area quickly he might cool down. Or at the very least he would become just another one of her creditors. Whom she couldn't pay, no matter how little the charge might be.

She turned on her heel and hurried back into her own car. The engine was still running. She shifted into first gear and moved off. There was a screech of metal as the shopping trolley was pulled out of *his* radiator and fell crashing on to the ground. Without a second look Leonie gunned the engine. Her tyres squealed as they took hold of the concrete. Smoke piled out of her exhaust. Black smoke, as usual. She came to a full stop at the turn where the car park met with Main Street, and managed another look out of her side-window. He was standing by his car with a piece of metal in his hands, almost as if he were crying.

Leonie started off again, almost creaming the furniture truck that appeared out of her line of vision. She jammed on her brakes and spent a moment or two catching her breath. He was probably responsible for it all anyway, she told herself. That was stupid, parking an antique car in a supermarket car park!

Charlie Wheeler looked at the bright chrome wire that he picked up from under his car, the remnant of the shopping trolley. There was something suspiciously like a tear in his eye. He loved the old antique. It had been a wreck when he bought it, and now it was a wreck again. He shuddered as he remembered those earlier bills. Not that he didn't have the money. The family was hardly broke. But there was always the principle of the thing!

He shook his head as he looked over the wreckage. But he had to go. There was another appointment he must keep, and Cecilia was an impatient little girl. Even her father quivered at the thought of a riled-up daughter. Nine years old, and she already qualified as the Dragon Lady! He fumbled with the door-handle of the car. His

battery-operated telephone was inside, locked between
the two front seats. The door was jammed. Disgusted,
he put one hand on the top of the door and vaulted over
the side. His ascent was good, but his landing left a little
to be desired. He managed to pull the telephone out and
rested it on the top of the map case. Another ten minutes
was required before he found the number of a tow shop.
A longer argument ensued when he tried to have the car
towed. And only the offer to rent a car from the same
garage seemed to bring action on the towing.

The sun was completely gone behind the Berkshires
by the time he managed both. The driver of the tow-
truck went off, shaking his head as he did so. Parts for
the Packard, he wanted Charlie to know, were hardly
available on a Friday night in Fairview, and in any case
the cost would be out the ears.

Charlie Wheeler was so glad to see him go that he
almost agreed to anything. When the tow-truck went by
him, his precious car riding a tow-tether at its back, he
shook his head and fumbled in his pocket for the card
Leonie Marshal had given him. It took him a minute or
so to focus his eyes to read.

'Hell and damnation,' he muttered. There was no address, no telephone number, no nothing on the card.
Just her name. Leonie Marshal, Fairview. He would need
a sheriff's posse to track her down.

Ordinarily he would be screaming bloody murder by
this time, he told himself, but instead he was chuckling.
The damn little minx! There would be a 'next time'.
There would absolutely be a 'next time'! That kiss was
too good to waste!

Four blocks north, Leonie had just finished the second
of her four remaining errands, and had come up to the
'stop' sign at the junction of Main Street, when the pro-

cession went by. A tow-truck, with the ancient Packard trailing behind, and a black threatening Porsche, with that man at the wheel. That man! Already she recognised him as an enemy, a threat to her precariously balanced economy. Without thinking she stuck her tongue out at him, and then hastily clapped her hand over her mouth, for fear he might see even in the gathering darkness. There's something behind that face of his, her mind acknowledged. Something that affected her strongly. But what?

The driver behind her sounded his horn; Leonie crashed her gears and hurried off to Shawmut Avenue, where the milk co-operative was already four weeks late with the monthly cheque.

CHAPTER TWO

CHARLIE WHEELER managed well enough in his rental car, a two-year-old black Porsche. He came out of the supermarket car park and found himself on Main Street, headed north. The address he wanted was 972 Main Street. It ought to be north, he told himself, and wheeled out into the traffic.

The traffic flow was light. The street was lined with a miscellany of empty and boarded-up stores. The road was bumpy enough to test his driving skill. As with most other small towns in western New England, the business district of Fairview had shut down forever, and business had moved to one of several malls on the outskirts of town.

The sun had already disappeared below the peaks of the Berkshires. A dim twilight, purple in the mottled sky, pervaded the world. One or two faint stars could be seen low on the horizon.

He checked his wristwatch as he went. Five-fifteen. He had left Cecilia at four o'clock at the playschool, with a promise of quick return. His daughter would be having fits by about this time. But his errand was vital. Gradually the houses faded away on both sides, until he was at the outskirts of town.

After an interval a big white house came up on his left. He slowed to reconstruct his mental notes. A big white farmhouse, set off from the road by a four-foot-high stone wall. A reddish-brown barn behind it, a large signpost shaped like a dairy cow and a spotlight bright enough to illuminate the whole entrance area. The sign was inscribed 'Fairview Farms'. A good many acres of land, rolling meadow land, ran behind the barn. Cows. It all seemed correct. He pulled over to the side of the road and sat for a minute, thinking he had found a place to re-start his organisation. Now all he needed was a home for himself and his daughter. And then the work could begin!

There was only one light on in the house, in the back, in what probably would be the kitchen. Charlie Wheeler, a man who had been raised in more than a couple of small towns, smiled as he started his engine, backed up a few paces, and turned into the dirt driveway that ran along the side of the house.

The back door opened as he pulled to a stop. The woman waiting for him was tall and white-haired, dressed in a faded dress and apron. She favoured her right leg, supporting it with an aluminium cane. She would probably not see sixty-five again, he judged, but she was full of vim and life.

'Mr Wheeler?' she called.

'Yes. Charlie Wheeler,' he assured her as he went up the stairs two at a time.

'Come in.' She stepped aside and ushered him into the kitchen. It was a big room, and by no means as old as the house itself.

He put out his hand. 'Mrs Stone?'

She chuckled and engaged his hand. 'I should be so lucky,' she said. 'Ms Stone. Or call me Aunt Agnes. Everyone else in town does.'

'I'm sorry to be so late. There was a little—accident down at the store. It's hard to believe the amount of bad luck that's been chasing me around town today.'

'Then perhaps you'll stay for supper while we talk?'

'I would like to, but my daughter is still waiting for me down at the playschool you recommended. That is, if she hasn't blown her top by now. I think perhaps I'll just make your acquaintance and be off.'

'That's no problem. I'll just make one telephone call, and everything will be taken care of.'

'Magician?'

'Well, when I was much younger people used to refer to me as "Witch". But that's long ago. The supper's ready, the table is set. All we need wait for is the rest of the family. Maybe you would like to see around the house in the meantime?'

'I'd love that.'

It was six forty-five before Leonie Marshal drove up to the house. The child beside her was a puzzle. She was big for her age, a stocky blonde with a round face and steel-blue eyes that seemed to glare perpetually. According to Martha, Leonie's assistant at the school, the child had spent the entire afternoon huddled in a corner of the classroom, refusing to talk to either students or adults.

Tight-lipped, she made no objection when told Leonie was taking her to her father, but passed the ride in silence.

'Hmm. We have company,' Leonie commented as she drove up and wedged her old car alongside the gleaming Porsche. 'Anybody you know?'

Cecilia sat up to get a good view out of the window. Then she shook her head and slouched down again.

'Well, this is as far as we go, child. Come along.'

Leonie was acting out one of the prime rules of single-child care. Act as if you expect the child to obey, and chances are good that they will. Cecilia did, sliding out of the passenger door and following along.

Aunt Agnes was standing by the kitchen table. 'Supper in ten minutes,' the old lady announced. She was staring down the hall at the bathroom. Leonie settled her glasses on her nose and turned to watch. Someone was coming out of the bathroom. A man. A big man.

'Oh, my God,' Leonie groaned.

'Oh, my God indeed,' Charlie Wheeler said. He reached inside the pocket of his blazer and pulled out the card Leonie had forced on him back in the car park. 'You didn't leave any forwarding address.'

Caught in her own trap, Leonie turned scarlet and fumbled for words. Which she didn't need. The little girl who had been almost hiding behind her came around in front. 'Daddy,' the child said, 'you promised to come at five o'clock. I'm mad at you.'

'I don't doubt it, child,' he said. 'Come over here and I'll tell you all about it.'

'So you see,' Charlie said, 'I had no better choice than to come to our only remaining store, set up a household for my daughter and me, and find us a home.' His daughter, standing behind him, squirmed around.

'I don't like it here,' she said.

'Of course,' Aunt Agnes said, paying no attention to the child's comment. There was a certain warmth in her voice, and a deep smile on her face. 'Certainly you had nothing else you could have done.'

'Will one of you people tell me what's going on?' Leonie interjected. Aunt Agnes was getting far too familiar with this—man. God knows, Leonie told herself, we're in bad enough straits, but my lovable old Aunt is liable to give the store away, as they say in Yankeeland.

'It's all very simple,' Aunt Agnes said as she moved back to the stove. 'Now you pull up chairs to the table. I have a quick meal, beef stew, and a pot of tea——'

'I don't like tea,' little Cecilia interrupted.

'Believe me, you'll like *this* tea.' Her father produced a threatening look. 'And the beef stew. You'll like that too. And you'll say "please" and "thank you" when you've finished. Right?'

The girl tucked her head into his shoulder, seemed to shudder for a moment, and then poked her head out, grim-faced. 'Right. Yes, thank you,' she muttered.

Aunt Agnes hustled them into chairs. All except Leonie. She stood to one side and watched Charlie's face as it went from commanding to accepting to enjoyment. And his daughter matched each facial movement.

'I think we had better scrub up,' Leonie suggested. 'The children were colouring this afternoon while I was out shopping. Cecilia?'

The girl docilely followed her down the hall to the downstairs bathroom and carefully closed the door behind them. 'Now look,' the girl said firmly, as if explaining a situation to a dunce. 'My dad is a nice man. I like him. We live together, he and I. I'm happy about that. I wouldn't want you to try to play footsie with my dad. I don't mind putting up with this nonsense for a day or two, but I wouldn't want you to feel you can move in on us. Got that?'

'This is the hot-water faucet,' Leonie said, flustered. 'And no, you don't have to worry about me horning in on your good life. Is *he* happy, by the way?'

'That's none of your business,' the girl said as she soaped her hands and rubbed them together.

And that, Leonie told herself, is the wise word direct from Pharaoh's daughter, eh? She started to add a wise word or two of her own, and gave up. They both came trailing up the corridor to where Aunt Agnes and Charlie Wheeler were making small talk around the table. The tureen of stew was set in the middle of the table.

Leonie, from force of habit, took the chair at the end and picked up the ladle. It was a thick, luxurious stew, crammed with potatoes and onions and carrots, with a blend of spices which could only be named by the cook.

'Good,' Charlie said as he moved on to his second spoonful.

'It's—all right,' his daughter chipped in. Her eyes were down at the plate, with not a bit of a look at Leonie.

'Best I've tasted in a monk's age,' Aunt Agnes averred. 'It couldn't possibly be better. Leonie does all the major cooking around here. She made this up this morning.' From that point onwards the conversation became generalised, with Cecilia paying no attention, and Leonie wishing that someone might throw her a bone of explanation now and again.

About halfway through the apple pie somebody said something that snapped Leonie up to attention.

'What did you say?' she demanded of Wheeler. She put down her spoon, leaving it to clatter on her blue rose plate, and put both elbows on the table.

'Ah, still with us?' he asked. 'Well, the office space that you use for your playschool is just about what I require for my store headquarters.'

'With one store you need a headquarters——?'

'Now Leonie,' her aunt interrupted.

'This is important, Aunt Agnes.' She turned her attention back to Wheeler. 'I suppose you know that I'm using the only clear area in the entire township? We need this playschool. With both mothers and fathers working these days, two-income families are very important. And I need the income. So who the devil are you to butt into our town and try to rearrange our needs?'

'I'm fully aware——' he started to say.

'Leonie.' Her aunt rapped the table once with a spoon. 'Mr Wheeler is our guest and will be so treated.'

'I should kiss him while he tries to steal our school? That's not right, Aunt.' And then, glaring across the table at her guest, 'And what makes you think you can break my lease?'

'Breaking your lease ought to be pretty easy,' he said. She watched him with cobra eyes as one hand slid into his coat pocket and came out with a handful of papers. He pulled one loose from the pile. 'Offices— where——' he muttered to himself. 'Ah, here we are. I see that I don't have to break your lease. It expired six months ago.'

'Oh, no,' Leonie groaned. 'I knew there was something I forgot to do. But surely Mr DeMello wouldn't mind restoring our lease. His daughter goes to our playschool. Both of them, for that matter.'

She flipped her heavy swath of hair in his general direction, passing on a speechless 'so there' look, and sat back in her chair, her arms folded across her capacious bosom.

'Leonie,' her aunt interrupted. 'Please. This is so embarrassing. Mr Wheeler seems to——'

'Not seems to,' Wheeler interrupted. 'Very definitely *has*. Charlie Wheeler, that scourge of Fairview town, has bought the building from our Mr DeMello. Now what do you think of that?'

What do I think of that? Miss Leonie Marshal had a half-bite of pie in her mouth, and his words choked her. She struggled for a moment, with anger fighting gravity, then bolted for the bathroom.

'Something I said?' Charlie Wheeler laid down his fork, wiped his lips, and listened intently to the retching noises coming from the bathroom.

'I suppose you had every right to say what you did,' Aunt Agnes said grimly. 'It *is* a free country.' She had become a tired old lady between two successive ticks of the old pendulum clock on the wall. 'But it did seem to me that you were going out of your way to make it hard on her. Her playschool brings in most of the money we have. And now if you expect she'll respond very nicely to your offer to buy the house and the farm—well, I think you have rocks in your head!'

'I don't mean to be the Big Bad Wolf,' Wheeler replied, 'but you two people happen to have in your control the two prime pieces of land I need to start back in business. I intend to rebuild this store; have no doubt about it. But one store is hardly enough. My grandfather had thirty-two. It's true that I'll make some of you discontent, but it's my intention to open up two hundred jobs or more in this little town. Does that make me the bad guy?'

'No,' Aunt Agnes said slowly. 'It doesn't make you the bad guy.'

'But it doesn't make you the good guy either,' his daughter told him. 'I wish we could eat like this all the time.'

'And that wise remark gives me another idea,' he said. 'Do you suppose, Aunt Agnes, that if I come around say at about—oh, nine o'clock tomorrow morning I could get to talk sensibly to your niece?'

'Tomorrow's Saturday. I can see that she's here,' the elderly lady replied. 'And I can see that you have an opportunity to talk to her, but nobody in God's green world could guarantee that Leonie Marshal will listen. And she's not my niece. We're really not related. Some day I'll explain it all to you.'

The next day crept soft and early into town. A breeze of less than five miles an hour stirred a few of the falling leaves. In the early morning the ducks were up, launching themselves into the southbound flyway, and chattering squirrels were hurrying their gathering. A farm dog howled in the distance, over towards Springfield.

Charlie Wheeler, all glass and glitter in his new rental Porsche, slowed down across the street from the Marshal house and gave it another look-see. In the early morning light it looked better than it had in the twilight of the evening before. He stepped out of his car and stretched his legs. His daughter, only half awake, wandered after him, holding one hand.

Finally satisfied, he backed his car into the driveway and parked it neatly so that the light truck ahead of him could have a clear way to the street.

Miss Stone—Agnes, he remembered—was waiting for him at the side-door. She ushered them into the kitchen and closed the screen door behind them.

'She's up?'

'Since five o'clock,' she informed him. 'Farm folk are always up and about rather earlier than city people. Have you had breakfast?'

'Not really,' he said. 'Fathers with daughters living in a hotel are also up and about. Not by five o'clock, of course—what the devil is that?'

'That's our milk co-operative truck, come to collect the morning milk cans. And I'm afraid that you've parked your car in just the wrong position. Such a nice car you have. The co-operative drivers tend to be a little careless about expensive cars.'

'Then before we have another argument about cars I'd better go move it. Breakfast say in about ten minutes?'

'More or less,' Aunt Agnes said. 'I'll start your breakfast. Let me see now: orange juice and coffee. Toast, or maybe two muffins. Eggs?' She paused and looked at him, begging guidance.

'Over easy,' he told her. 'And sausages, if you have them. If not perhaps a slice of ham?'

'Perhaps we'll have both,' she said, laughing as a slight colouring of embarrassment added a solid hue to his bony face.

'I don't want to eat you out of house and home,' he said, but his smile confirmed his wants.

'You won't eat me out of house and home,' she insisted. 'After all, you have no idea how much over-market you're paying.'

'Did—Leonie—was she upset when she heard I wanted to buy the farm as well?'

'I didn't dare tell her. That part of the dirty work you'll have to take care of yourself. And remember, Leonie owns the whole place, bag and baggage.'

'I don't want to make it hard on her.'

'There's nothing you can do that will make it *easy* on my girl. We have a lot of troubles. The rates are going sky-high. The town is running a sewer line out along this road, and every resident has to pay a part of the assessed fee. And the milk—well, I'd better leave that to Leonie to explain. If she feels like it.'

'That's a kick in the head, Ms——'

'Call me Aunt Agnes,' she insisted. 'And get your car moved before the milk truck tries to come in. Believe me, they are the worst drivers in the county.'

'I know one who's worse,' he said as he dashed for the door.

'Smart alec,' Aunt Agnes said softly as she watched him through the window. Whatever else he might be, he was a skilful driver. It was hard not to feel a warmth for the man.

Leonie came up from the barn feeling worn to the bone. Milking the cows, moving the cans, feeding the animals, putting them out to pasture, cleaning the stalls, sterilising the milking machines, scouring out the newly returned milk cans—it was a seven-day-a-week job which left her back just a bit out of whack, and her temperament sixty degrees above equanimity. So she walked up to the house head down, dragging her mind. And as a result she missed the Porsche, carefully tucked into the corner of the building behind the back porch.

'Tired, love?'

'Broken back,' Leonie agreed. 'Thank God it's Saturday. What we need is a big strong male around the house.'

'Do you know, I was thinking exactly the same thing? Tea or coffee this morning?'

'I believe I'll have coffee. My, those pancakes smell good. Are we having guests for breakfast? I'd better get washed up. So who do you know that's a big broth of a man and wouldn't mind throwing a milk can or two occasionally for practically no wages?' And at that moment Leonie's eyes went to the far end of the table.

'Cecilia? What are you doing at our table?'

'My daddy said I ought to come over here for breakfast before I go off to school.'

'Your daddy...?' Leonie's face turned red as she gave thought. 'Your daddy said you ought to have breakfast with us—why isn't that nice? Of course, it's Saturday, and none of the schools will be open. Not even our playschool. The regular school year begins in about two weeks, doesn't it? Well, I'm glad to welcome you. Now, as I said, I'd best wash up and——'

'Perhaps you ought to wait,' Aunt Agnes interjected.

'You can't go in the bathroom.' Cecilia was so excited that she bounced up and down on her chair.

'I can't go in the bathroom?'

'Well, she can now.' Charlie Wheeler came out into the hall rolling down his sleeves.

'You!'

'Me. How's the breakfast coming, Aunt Agnes?'

'Coming along real fine, Charles. Take that seat at the head of the table.'

'Take that—my lord, is he moving in on us too?'

'Yes,' Cecilia said. 'Ain't you lucky?'

'You never said a truer word.' Leonie managed to squeeze out the words sarcastically. 'You own a complete store, and you have to eat at my table?'

'Leonie!' Aunt Agnes gazed directly into her niece's eyes and stared her down. Leonie tried to maintain her anger, and failed. She pulled up a chair and sat down, her face a mottled grey and red.

Aunt Agnes huffed a couple of times, and then settled back into her usual austere complexion.

'There is a great deal you don't understand,' her aunt continued. 'You know you told me if I had the strength I could open up a few of our rooms for bed and breakfast?' Her niece started to object but was overridden.

'I know it's rather sudden, but I've rented two rooms upstairs to Mr Wheeler. One for himself, and one for his daughter. He's paying the going rates, of course.'

'You mean——'

'Leonie, there is nothing wrong with your hearing. You know just what I mean. You'll remember that our agreement makes me the accountant and business manager. I consider that the subject is closed.'

'But——'

'Leonie!'

A deep quiet settled in, with only the occasional whuffing of the ancient hound dog, trying to settle down beneath the stove and at the same time catch every morsel that escaped fork and table. The morning was turning into a dismal clan meeting until finally the dog came over to Cecilia's knee and licked a spot where juice prevailed.

And at that moment the meeting turned into a game, known only to Cecilia and Leonie, and not at all notice-able to Aunt Agnes and Charlie.

'What the devil are you grinning about?' Charlie finally asked.

'Nothing. Nothing.' The girl giggled. 'It's a very good meal. Especially the hash-brown potatoes. The best I've had in a long time. Did you make it, Ms Stone?'

'Yes, love. Breakfast is the easy meal. I make that. Leonie makes all the other meals, like that stew we had last night. You liked that, didn't you?'

The little girl sat solemnly straight, not an expression on her face, as if she was examining the question from all sides. 'Yes,' she finally agreed. 'That was a good meal. But it can't be that good all the time.'

'Cecilia!'

Aunt Agnes patted Charlie's hand. 'The truth will out, Mr Wheeler. Ever since I retired from schoolteaching and Leonie took me in, Leonie has been the cook in our family. And the baker—and the planner.'

'Let me get this straight. You mean you two are not related?'

'No, we're only related through kindness——'

'She's my aunt Agnes,' Leonie interrupted them. 'We needed each other. We still do.'

'Altogether a woman for all seasons, huh?'

Leonie ducked her head away, hiding her blushing face under her swath of long hair. The meal went on. There was more laughter than suspicion; more warmth than grievance. And when it was done Aunt Agnes stood up and announced, 'And since Leonie and Charlie have done all the work, Cecilia and I will clear the table and start the dishwasher, while you two take a small walk for your stomachs' sake.'

Cecilia, with a considerable frown on her face, scraped back her chair. 'I have homework——' she started to say.

'Cecilia! School doesn't start for two weeks. How could you possibly have homework?'

'But I *do*, Dad. I'm in grade school, not just that silly after-school playschool thing. I have lots of things I have to review from my last school.'

'She's right, of course,' Aunt Agnes said. 'But then again we have a modern dishwasher, and tomorrow things might be switched around backwards, my dear.'

'You mean my father might have to do the dishes tomorrow?'

'It's entirely possible.'

'That's our cue,' Charlie said as he came around the table and took Leonie's hand. One gentle tug brought her out of her chair, and left her tagging along behind him.

'Better take a sweater,' Aunt Agnes called after them. 'It's well into autumn already.'

Moments later, outside under a full but chilled sun, he said, 'I've got a car here, you know. We could take a ride if you're not a mind to go walking.'

Leonie chuckled, still half enveloped in the sleeves of her boxy red sweater. When her mouth came free she was still laughing. 'When Aunty says walk, we walk. If Aunty feels we've not had enough exercise, she'll say, Run.'

'And what if your aunt said, Go smooch?'

'You should live so long.'

'Ah. A challenge?'

'If you think so.'

He gently tucked her arm in the crook of his and began to tow her away from the front of the house. She froze, but had barely the strength to keep him from moving her. They swayed back and forth like two dancers in a stately minuet. After a moment or so, her defences collapsed. He wheeled her around until she was facing him, not more than inches apart.

'And what do you think comes next?' she panted.

'I'd suggest that you give up.'

'Not before I scream. There are a couple of houses with telephones about five hundred yards down the street. If it hasn't come to your attention, Mr Wheeler, I don't like you. And I particularly don't like what you're trying to do to us.'

'Well, I don't think you have the slightest idea what I'm trying to do to you. I suggest you give your neighbours a blast,' he said as he pulled her forward directly into contact with his brown leather jacket. She took a deep breath and suddenly her mouth was sealed as his lips came down gently but firmly on hers.

For a moment she managed a gurgle, nothing more. She opened her mouth, and found his tongue blocking the way. A moment's struggle, gradually weakening, left her welded against his body, with no ability to fight him off. In fact the strength bled out of her in one involuntary gusty sigh, and she clung to him in pure desperation.

The kiss went on to indeterminable time and distance. What seemed like forever was, of course, barely a minute at most. And when he broke the contact she hung on to him with both hands clutching his shoulders. He lifted his head and buried his lips deep into her hair, and then nipped her earlobe gently. 'Nice scream,' he murmured into her ear.

'Oh, shut up,' she gasped at him. Her arms trembled, and her hands refused to turn him loose. She came back down off her toes, resting her weight on her heels, her head cushioned over his heart.

'Do you always have such a strong pulse?' Her head was turned to one side, with her left ear directly over the beat of his heart.

'Not lately,' he returned. 'In fact, never before. Shall we try that again?'

She didn't answer, but made no struggle when he pulled her back on tiptoes, accepted the help of both her arms, and began the ritual all over again. Close but gentle. Lips to lips, soft and caressing, hearing the music of the stars as she joined him again. And only then did she begin to struggle—until finally he said, 'Are you crying?'

'Don't be silly,' she said. 'It's raining!'

'That was a quick shower.' Aunt Agnes met them at the door with a half-raised umbrella.

'Wasn't it ever.' Leonie squeezed past her aunt to get shelter from the rain. She had thrown her hair back over her shoulder and her eyes were full of something more than raindrops, an item not entirely missed by her elderly aunt.

His daughter was waiting in the kitchen, somewhat withdrawn from the welcome. He came over and picked her up, swinging her around him and kissing her nose.

'You didn't know enough to come in out of the rain,' the girl said.

He tickled her under her ribs, and broke her out of her solemnity. 'And for that remark, young lady, off you go to settle into your new room!'

She rode on his shoulders the way a mahout might do on an elephant, until he tumbled her down on the bed in the guest room and let her bounce a time or two. He pulled back the curtain at her window, gave her one more kiss, and walked down into the living-room.

'We have this thing,' he said as he came in. 'She's discovered that she's a girl and I'm not, so no more helping her with her clothes, or with her bath, or—well, I'm sure you understand.'

'You've had her in custody for a long time?' Aunt Agnes watched him like a hawk.

'Not so's you'd notice,' he returned. 'My wife and I separated about six years ago, but Cecilia was only three years old, and stayed with her mother. I was pretty busy. In fact, I was hardly a weekend father. And then six months ago I was in an auto accident, and when I got back on my feet again my wife Carol had done a disappearing act, leaving Cecilia with my grandfather.'

'So you are, so to speak, an apprentice father?'

'Lady, you can say that again. And I don't even know the rules of the game. But I'm going to learn, believe me.'

I believe you, Leonie told herself. I'm sure you'll learn. But I wonder if you'll include any loving in your learning?

'Maybe I'd better go upstairs and supervise this bathing,' she suggested as she pushed her chair back from the table. 'Why don't you have another cup of coffee with my aunt?'

Charlie Wheeler had a doubting look on his face as he watched Leonie trudge up the stairs. 'I should have qualified my warning. She doesn't take on any men at all, and not many females.'

'Not to worry,' Aunt Agnes said. 'Leonie has the best track record in all the world. She can handle any child, from four to forty. Come along and let's have that other cup of coffee.'

'Well,' he murmured, 'believe me, I can use all the help I can get!'

CHAPTER THREE

SATURDAY afternoon. The heavy screen door slammed twice as Charlie Wheeler came back into the house. Leonie was sitting at the kitchen table, a pile of papers scattered around her.

'They found a horse,' Charlie said, chuckling. 'An old brown sway-back thing that Cecilia thought she could ride.'

'That'll be Dandy,' Leonie said as she looked up. 'He's twenty-five years old. My father bought him for me when I was three years old. I treasure him more than most things. He doesn't mind being friendly, but he doesn't have the energy to carry anybody around any more.'

'What are you up to? You look worried.'

'Who wouldn't be?' she said, sighing. 'Aunt Agnes just gave me the monthly figures. The price of milk on the retail market goes up, and the price of milk to those of us who raise it goes down. You know much about milk?'

'You bet. We used to sell five thousand gallons a week.'

'At what price?'

'I really don't remember. Explain the problem.'

Leonie reached over under her calculator and pulled out a sheet of paper. 'Look at this. It costs me thirteen fifty a hundredweight to produce the milk. If I'm lucky I get to sell it at twelve nineteen. The State provides a temporary subsidy that brings it up to fifteen dollars a hundredweight. But that's only temporary, and I only collect that months *after* the sale. And every time the state legislature meets up on Beacon Hill they start to

41

tinker with the price support for my milk. And only God can stop them. They're all lawyers, up there on the Hill. Not a farmer among them!'

'I don't understand about this hundredweight business.'

'It's just a unit of measure. Amounts to about nine liquid gallons, so to speak.'

'And you're losing money on every gallon?'

'More than even I know,' Leonie said quietly. 'I don't have the smarts to factor in all the twelve-hour days, or the interest on the loan on the meadow land, or the increase in grain prices. Or the cost of the new sewer system. I can't grow all my own fodder. I can get some hay off the swamp marshes, but to make milk my cows need grain. I'm just tied up in knots. I can't even pay the man who takes the bull down to the cows!'

'You need a man?'

For just once she mustered up a smile. 'No. A man isn't really important. It's the bull that I need.'

'Do I detect a little sarcasm there?'

'Just a little. Lord, I'm so darn tired. Every day I get more and more worn, more and more behind. The only things around here that make a profit are the school and the chickens. And you——'

'Yes,' he said bleakly. 'And I'm going to close out your school in two weeks.'

She stared up at him, dropped her papers, and leaned back in her chair. He could almost see a tear running down behind her heavy glasses. 'In two weeks? You don't give me much time, do you?'

'No. Time is an imperative. You don't have any idea how to improve things around the farm?'

'Temporary ideas,' she murmured. 'There's nothing to be said about the school. It's dead. You've killed it. All I can do is wind it up. That includes repaying the parents who paid tuition in advance. I don't have a red cent left for that repayment. And now I have twenty-three cows out there, eating me out of house and home. I suppose I could auction them off and shut down the dairy. God, I'd hate to do that. Still, I can't continue with these losses. Thank God that the house mortgage was paid off fifty years ago. I might go back to the bank and see what they'll offer on a new mortgage.'

'How's the market for cows?'

'Terrible.'

'And your chance of getting a mortgage on the house?'

'Slim. Worse than the market for cows.'

'Would you listen to an idea?'

'I'd listen to anything so long as it's not illegal or immoral.'

'Then why don't you sell everything—the cows, the house, the farm?'

'That's a great suggestion. I might make enough money so Aunt Agnes and I could live for—perhaps five years. Where I don't know. The town has some subsidised housing, but the waiting list is ten miles long. And then what? Besides, our chance of selling at a profit is minuscule. Most of the dairies all over the state have already gone under. Who would buy in the middle of a depression?'

'I would.'

'You?'

'Me.'

She whirled around to face him, anger mounting on her face. Her stomach roiled. You've been a fool, she told herself as she squared her shoulders and stood up. 'So that's the gimmick,' she snapped. 'You'll force me into a bankruptcy sale, and then have the whole ball of wax! I might have known! First you buy my school out of existence, and now you want to buy out my dairy!'

'And the house too,' he said, nodding his head.

'Lock, stock and damn barrel?'

'Exactly.'

Leonie slowly rose to her feet. Her cheeks, once red with anger, had faded away into a white sheen. 'You'd do all that to me? Why? Just because I wrecked your car? Your old car?'

'My antique car,' he insisted solemnly. 'And no, my antique car has nothing to do with it.'

'I—don't understand you. I thought for a moment there that you—cared about us. Now I see that you don't. In fact, I have the feeling that you hate us. Us and the whole town, perhaps! Are you trying to get even with us for all your troubles?'

Charlie Wheeler took a couple of steps, his left hand half extended in her direction, petitioning. She backed off until her thighs ran into the table. 'Don't you touch me,' she snarled. 'Not a finger.'

He froze in position, and then brushed his black hair out of his eyes. There was a gleam of pain in their dark depths. Leonie, with her back half turned to him, did not see it.

'I didn't say that very well, did I?' He shrugged his shoulders, disgusted at himself.

'Oh, I thought you said it all very well. Right to the point. The only problem is that I'm not selling. And you can move out of my house as soon as possible, if you please.'

'No, I can't do that,' he said bleakly. 'I have to provide a home for my daughter. Until I find a house for us, I'm staying here. I signed a one-month contract with your aunt for bed and breakfast. I intend to hold you to it.'

'You don't have any feeling of shame? It doesn't bother you to have to live in a house with two women whom you intend to throw out in the street?'

'That's not exactly what——'

'You don't care how much I hate you? How much I am upset just by your presence?'

'I care,' he said softly, 'but I don't intend to let it change my mind.'

'Then there's nothing more we have to say to each other. Just keep out of my way.' She turned back to the table and gathered all her papers in an untidy heap. She took one more good look at him, and then whirled away to hide her tears.

Back in her room she dumped the papers on her bed and slumped down beside them. Her shoulders shook as she fought off the tears. For just a day or two she had known him. Just a day or two, and he had walked into her heart. You're lucky, she told herself. What would it be like if he really wormed his way in, all the way? Jeff Littler all over again?

There wasn't time to mourn. Jeff had taken three months to work her around. And then, the week before the wedding, had walked off with her bank book and every cent of cash the house contained. This—man—did all the hurting in forty-eight hours. Leonie Marshal, what a double-dyed fool you are. No more men, Leonie. Do you hear that? No more men!

Somebody knocked at her bedroom door. Leonie came up off the bed like a rocket.

'Leonie? It's me—Aunt Agnes. What do you want to do about supper tonight?' Aunt Agnes was holding something in her hand. She was distracted. Leonie knew she hadn't knocked on the door to ask about dinner. Aunt Agnes had some bad news for her.

For just a moment Leonie Marshal wanted to throw off all her obligations. She didn't want any more bad news. Let them all scrounge for themselves. Or go hungry!

But Aunt Agnes was a diabetic, and required four well-balanced meals every day. And that—man—was as thin as a rail and required feeding up. And then there was the girl. Swiftly Leonie dashed away the tears, fumbled in her top draw for a clean handkerchief, and vainly brushed her mass of curls off her face. She knew she was clinging to excuses. She was getting gun-shy about news but she asked anyway, 'Did the postman bring any mail?'

'Yes, dear,' Aunt Agnes said. 'But I don't think you really want this letter. It's from Cedar Junction, the state's maximum security prison.'

'Oh, God! Jeff Littler again?' She put out her hand and Aunt Agnes reluctantly dropped the pencilled letter into it.

Leonie turned the envelope over a couple of times, but could read nothing on the outside. She tore the letter open with her thumbnail. It contained a single page, scrawled in pencil, almost illegible. Her face paled, and she crumpled it up.

'What?' Aunt Agnes asked.

'He wants us to know that his term is being shortened because of good behaviour.'

'Oh, my. Him? Good behaviour?'

'And he wants me to know he's coming directly back to Fairview when he gets out!'

'How can they do that?' Aunt Agnes gasped.

'I don't know,' Leonie murmured. 'You remember at the court trial, what he promised he would do to me when he got out?' Leonie was hanging on to her composure for all it was worth.

'Can he come back here?' Aunt Agnes asked anxiously.

'Maybe we could get a restraining order,' Leonie suggested. 'Well, it's no use worrying about it until they turn him out. I hope he thinks twice about it,' she added. 'Why don't you go back downstairs? I'll be along to start the dinner in a minute.'

The hall and the kitchen seemed to have been swept clean, as if everyone else in the house was going out of their way to avoid her. Leonie shrugged. They needed her; she didn't need him—them. She could hear the voices from the living-room. Charlie speaking, Aunt Agnes laughing, and an occasional little titter from Cecilia.

The pork shoulder had already been boned. In fact Tighe, the family dog, was gnawing on the bone over in the corner, seeming very pleased with the world. Leonie, who loved the dog hardly less than she loved her horse, felt bereft. Nobody loves *me*, she assured herself as she mixed the stuffing and began to set up the evening meal.

When the wall clock struck five Leonie could hear the others come in from all over the house. The table was set in the dining-room, a complete change from normal. She and Aunt Agnes regularly ate in the kitchen. After a moment her aunt came out to investigate.

'Only three places set, Leonie? Want me to finish the settings?'

'No. I'm having my meal in the kitchen.'

'That's childish, Leonie.'

'Is it really?'

'Now don't give me the arched eyebrows, miss. You're not eating with us just to prove to him that you're still angry.'

'Well, I hope he can see that as easily as you can.'

'Leonie!'

Leonie turned her back. It was far and away an unusual thing. Although Aunt Agnes was really not a
relative, Leonie had come to love her in the six years
they had been together. And yet—— Mr Charles Wheeler
was something larger than a pain in the neck. He was
positively a negative; somehow she had to get rid of him.
But right now there were other things to do.

Leonie snatched up a carving knife and engineered a
roast pork sandwich. There was a moment of debate in
her mind. From the dining-room everyone seemed to be
full of good cheer. Even Cecilia's giggle punctuated the
conversation. But a chair was scraping back. Someone
was bound to come and enquire. Leonie snatched up the
sandwich and fled to her bedroom.

By ten o'clock all the others had gone to bed, but
Leonie's problems were still booming inside her head.
Her bedroom was too confining for her. She picked up
all her papers, as well as her lap-top computer, and stole
out into the dining-room. It was a cool night, and she
was still dressed in her long flannel polka-dot granny
gown. She had owned it for five years or more, and while
it was still the same size she was not. It fitted somewhat
tightly around the bodice and across her hips. But it was
warm, and it was comfortable, and the house was silent.
The dining-room was practically empty. Just a big, highly
polished table, big enough to sit twelve, a couple of
marble-top sideboards along the far wall for crockery,
a small electric chandelier in the ceiling that once had
held candles, and a pair of floor lamps. There was room
on the big table to spread out, and she did.

She worked slowly. Not for the Leonies of this world
the high-speed thinking, the quick analysis. Aunt Agnes,
who could lasso and tame any set of figures in record
time, had made her a summary. And now it was up to
Leonie to come to some decision. She was caught

unawares when the wall clock in the hall struck twelve. She pushed back her chair and stretched mightily. All the muscles in her shoulders ached from being too long in one cramped position. They were more accustomed to the easy swing of loaded milk cans. All those papers on the table had been reduced to six, each stacked with figures a mile long. She had only to tally them up, consider, and make her decision. It sounded so easy; almost like jumping off the top of the Washington Monument. She gave herself a shake, like some hungry cat, and reached for the pile of papers again.

The coffee-cup rattled in its saucer, and the smell tugged at her nostrils. 'Thank you, Aunt Agnes,' she murmured without looking up.

'You're entirely welcome,' the deep voice at her elbow said. Her hand, stealing towards the handle of the cup, jumped away, startled. The cup rattled again. A tiny portion of the hot coffee came up over the rim and burned the thick pad of flesh on her forefinger.

'Damn,' she muttered as she sucked on the finger.

'At least that,' he returned. 'Are you finished?'

She forgot for a moment all her anger at this man. 'Not quite,' she said, sighing. 'I have to total these all up and then I can see where I am.'

'Cute little thing,' he said as he sat down beside her. Her head snapped up. 'The computer,' he told her defensively. He swept the little instrument over in front of him, gathered the six papers to be totalled, flexed his fingers, and the computer began to jump at his command.

Leonie watched in amazement. Only a mediocre computer operator herself, she knew she was in the presence of some sort of wizard. His fingers flew at the maximum speed of the electronic marvel. Five minutes passed. Leonie stared at him.

'There you go.' He shoved the computer back towards her. 'Not a pretty picture.' He hummed as he figured. There was a boyish expression on his face, as if he enjoyed the doing more than the conclusions.

'You—you've done some computer work?'

'I guess you could say that. Not on the likes of this little baby, but there it is. I went to a school that taught computers.'

'A trade school?'

'I—think they'd be a little insulted at the name, but yes, a trade school. It's called the Massachusetts Institute of Technology.'

'I'm not in the mood to have you pull my leg!' She swivelled her chair away from him and brushed her hair back. A trade school! Hah! MIT, the aristocratic East Coast leader in all technological research. 'You must think me some kind of back-country idiot!'

'Nice legs,' he replied. 'Which one of them should I pull?'

'Neither,' she snapped. 'Thank you. Go away.'

'Just when I'm beginning to be useful?'

Leonie grabbed both arms of her chair and pushed herself to a stand. 'Now look——'

'What a good idea,' he murmured as his hands fell to her shoulders.

'I said——'

'You said "now look",' he replied. 'I'm looking.' His arms pulled her closer. She tried to struggle, but only momentarily. Her head rested on his chest, just under his chin. Despite her opinion of the fellow, it was a very—comforting—place to be. Without thought she turned her head sideways and cuddled closer. The beat of his heart thundered in her ear, like a primitive call to—to what?

'Don't do that,' she muttered as she came to her senses. The pressure of his arms went slack, but she stayed in position for a moment. Just enough to gather her strength, she told herself. Even though I don't need any strength to break away from him. A pregnant pause. Move, she commanded her wayward feet. Her toes jiggled. 'Move,' she commanded, aloud this time, and desperately. Her feet inched backwards. Just far enough backwards to be free of his chest, no further.

'That's far enough,' he murmured in her ear. One of his big index fingers came down under her chin and tilted it up. His head seemed to fill her vision. There was a wondrous smile on his face, and it was coming closer.

Leonie made one of those lightning decisions that a girl sometimes made. She could either back away or slap him. And having reviewed both alternatives she shrugged her shoulders, closed her eyes, and waited to see what would happen. It was not what she expected.

His warm, moist lips touched on her forehead, then skipped gently down to the tip of her nose, and finally made contact with her own lips. There was no startling crash of emotion. It felt—comfortable. For one tense moment she stood stiffly in his arms. And then, surrendering to the calm comfort, she relaxed against him. His lips teased her, tested her, and then withdrew.

She felt warm and sleepy. Her eyelids were heavy beyond compare. His huge hands returned to her shoulders and pushed her gently away. She stood flat-footed, and struggled with those troublesome eyelids. A moment later she managed a blink. His face was just a few inches away. His huge dark eyes were full of twinkling enjoyment.

'There,' he said gruffly, 'that wasn't so bad, was it?'

It was the wrong thing to say. Kiss and tell? she asked herself as she worked up her anger. Does he think he

can wash away all the troubles he's causing just by a
little seduction? Gentle seduction? Her cheeks turned
blush-red as the anger swelled.

He made his second mistake: his smile turned into a
grin. He moved one hand up and traced the course of
the kiss, first to her forehead, then trailing down on to
her button nose, down to her mouth. Leonie's eyes
blinked closed again. His finger continued, down around
the curve of her chin. And then it jumped to the pointed
tip of her breast, which filled out the form and fashion
of her nightgown. He pushed gently with one finger, as
if he were ringing a doorbell.

The shock was enough to wash away the haze. Her
eyes flew open. He was grinning, a warm, friendly grin.
For the first time she recognised that she wore only that
long nightgown. It was as opaque as any ballroom dress,
nevertheless it was a nightgown. She was standing inches
away from this—man—dressed only in her nightgown,
and he had one hand on her breast, toying with it as if
it were his own property. Calvinistic Leonie Marshal
would have no part of that. She mustered her strength
and bounced her right palm off his cheek, just adjacent
to that grin. All the muscles built up by her dairy training
were behind that swing. The contact sound echoed
throughout the room. His smile disappeared.

Charlie Wheeler backed off a foot or two, his hand
fingering his damaged cheek gently. 'No, huh?'

'No, never,' she spat at him. She could almost see the
imprint of her hand on his reddened cheek. As quickly
as her anger had risen, so equally did it disappear. She
was never a girl to bear a grudge, and it came to her
suddenly that he was still a partially disabled man.

Her own palm stung. No matter what he was physi-
cally, he was a big, solid man. Embarrassed, she caught
her hands behind her, fingers entwined, not sure just

what to do next. He spared her the decision. That tantalising smile came back and he moved a step nearer. Leonie drew in her breath in a whistling gasp, her eyes mesmerised by his, her mind spinning. She backed away, only to come up solidly against the back of her chair. 'Don't you dare,' she muttered, having no idea what this arrogant male just might try.

'Dare?'

'Never.' She was holding her breath, and having difficulties doing so.

'You believe in lying?'

'I never lie.'

'I'm glad to hear that. You enjoyed that little kiss!'

'I——' You did, you know you did, she told herself. But I certainly can't tell him that! No telling what he might do.

'Convicted by your own silence,' he said chuckling.

Leonie stiffened and shook her head. Her long hair swirled around her heart-shaped face, giving her some hiding space.

'We'll see,' he announced.

Leonie wasn't exactly seeing. Her eyes were half closed, and her hair was screening him out. So his next move was a surprise. His big hands gently snatched away her glasses.

Leonie's world went out of focus. Oh, she could see the body form of him, and his size. She could see the brilliant lamp standing by the marble-top sideboard on the far side of the room. She could see through the open kitchen door, and into the kitchen itself, still brightly lit. And then, as she dithered, there was no need to see anything at all.

She was wrapped in his arms, pulled tightly against his chest, with no capacity to wiggle or fight—even if she had wanted to. He kissed her. Not something warm and comforting, but rather a smashing attack on all her senses as impulses went shooting up and down her spine, and her mind lost control entirely of the goings-on.

'That's my girl,' he said some hours later. 'And that's what it's really all about.'

Leonie, lying there in his arms, tried to catch her breath. It hadn't been temporal hours, she knew; in fact it might only have been a minute or two. But the effect had been a total bombardment of all her senses that seemed to go on and on forever. One more attack like that, she knew, would leave her totally malleable in his hands. A terrible thing to look forward to, but she was unable to convince her muscles that there was any threat, any reason to break away. Maybe, she told herself as she tried to suppress the sirens ringing in her mind, maybe he'll do it again.

But he didn't.

Back in her room, with the door securely locked, Leonie Marshal tried her best to reassemble all her thoughts. He hadn't kissed her again. Not a burning shaking kiss like that last one. Instead he had set her carefully back down in her chair and brushed her mass of hair out of her eyes.

She had sat rigidly in the chair, like some big puppet, waiting for him to pull on her strings. He'd bent over and kissed her gently on her forehead, and then carefully affixed her glasses just on the tip of her nose. Carefully she'd lifted a finger and pushed the spectacles further up. The world had come into focus. She'd taken a deep breath and then slowly scanned the room. She had not been entirely alone. The family dog had come in to investigate. He had stood there with his cold nose on her knee, his tail wagging slowly. And Charlie Wheeler had been nowhere to be seen.

She had scrambled to pick up all her papers, and then, clutching her lap-top computer in one hand, had fled to the relative safety of her bedroom. The dog was too old to keep up. He'd wobbled up to the closed door and sat down in the hall to mourn.

Inside Leonie was doing much the same. She dumped all her paperwork on her bed and sat down in her rocking-chair. It was an old comfort, this rocking-chair, back and forth, back and forth, with a little squeak each time the rocker went over the near edge of the rug which her grandmother had braided so many years before. She wrapped her arms across her breasts as she rocked. What about him?

He was big and strong and—skinny, but that was something time would cure. There were devils in his dark eyes. He was well-educated, but not in the handling of grocery chains. He was married and divorced, and must have been hell to live with. And his daughter was not far behind him.

And yet there was something about him, some half-hidden charm. She remembered the reactions of the people in the store. And Aunt Agnes, who judged people with cold caution, had evidently decided that he was the best thing to come down the pike since sliced bread!

Luckily I know what he is, Leonie told herself. Otherwise he'd sweep us all in a heap and by this time next week he'd own the house and we'd be living in the streets! And maybe he still would, her conscience assured her, unless she fought him tooth and nail.

She shrugged. Her room was getting cooler. A rain storm had come up and was beating on the plastic screens of her window. And on the bed beside her were all those papers. Leonie brought her chair to a halt and got up to find a robe.

The dog was still mourning. Leonie went to the door and unbolted it. 'Come in,' she murmured, 'before you wake the whole house.'

The dog scooted by her. Too old to vault on to the bed, he circled himself a time or two on the rug, rested his head on his forelegs.

'Tighe,' she said, sighing, 'I don't know what to do. There's some furniture in the school, not much, but a little something. No help there. In my own bank account there's a mere six hundred dollars. And the cheque from the milk co-operative isn't due until the tenth of the following month.' Her dog looked at her with those liquid brown eyes, and yawned.

'Thank you for your close attention,' she commented, as Tighe closed his eyes and abandoned her. She picked up the summary papers again.

Carefully she scanned the column of figures, hoping that Aunt Agnes's maths were in error. But they weren't. She turned away from the bed and walked over to the window. The rain pattered against the glass. She leaned her forehead against the window-pane and found some peace in the misty coolness.

There was no way out. The playschool had to close. Tomorrow she would have to make the announcement, and then call all the parents. But where could she find the money to pay them all off?

Leonie paced back to the bedside again and dug out the second sheet of totals on the dairy. There was no way to realise the money in two weeks, but perhaps she could borrow temporarily from some place, and then sell off the dairy, cows and all. And then?

Like some sort of android she began to pick up all the scattered papers and pile them atop her bureau. Her dog opened one eye and whined at her. She bent down to pat his ancient head, and then climbed into the bed.

Her light flashed out, the yellow glare instantly replaced by the faded shadows of the rainy night coming through the unshaded window. She stretched herself out flat on her back.

Sell Dandy? she asked herself. Don't be a fool. Who would want to buy a twenty-five-year-old horse? And how could she, who loved him so much, survive without him? Nonsense!

Sell it all, she told herself, struggling against the tears. Her legs were trembling. She stiffened in position. It's a terrible year. The town is in the depths of a serious depression. But I'm a healthy woman. Sell it all. Cows and machinery and—but not Dandy. Sell everything else. Surely there's something I can find to do to support us? There *has* to be something I can do!

But nothing came to mind.

Her thoughts rambled back to her childhood, when Grandpa had sat up late at nights with exactly the same problem. She tugged the blankets and pulled them over her head. In the dark tunnel of the night surely nothing could get her? In her mind's eye a tremendous form loomed over her. Charlie Wheeler, clothed in loincloth and knife, waving his hands about as if trying to find and seize her. She cringed and, semi-dreaming, Leonie Marshal fell into a troubled sleep.

CHAPTER FOUR

COME Monday morning Leonie was late. All her usual parking spaces, scattered along First Street, were full. But it was a sunny day, with high puffs of tiny white clouds scudding along under the influence of a gusting wind. There was the brisk tang of autumn and burning leaves in the air.

Nobody had been up back at the farmhouse. Aunt Agnes had been fast asleep when Leonie peeked in on her. Cecilia's room was empty. Her father's bedroom door was wide open. Leonie had wavered outside in the corridor for a moment, and then stuck her head around the door-jamb. The man had gone, his bed carefully made up, and everything picked up. Leonie, whose room always looked as if a tornado had struck it, had felt just the least bit guilty.

Bed and breakfast, the pair of them had engaged for. There was no sign that they had eaten. Leonie had managed a quick cup of coffee for herself and prepared to leave. Her dog Tighe, a polite male if ever there was one, had stirred and escorted her to the back door. The wind had whipped at her skirts. Being the schoolmistress required some formality. A navy blue skirt, knee-length, a lace-ruffled white blouse, and a heavy leather jacket to match autumn's temperature; all this served the dignity of her position. Her lush, heavy fall of hair, all braided and fastened into a chignon at the base of her neck, added a pair of years to her age. She had smiled at herself as she'd passed by the mirror fastened by the door. A solemn woman-of-the-world, it had told her, but Leonie was never one to take such things seriously.

Behind the closed door Tighe had offered one brief yip and was quiet. And probably gone promptly back to sleep, Leonie had told herself as she'd manoeuvred her old car through the confusion of the barn-yard and up on to the street.

She ended up parking on South Second Street, about four blocks from the playschool. There were few people out and about. The only real activity on these downtown streets came from banks and bankers, and a handful of grocery shoppers and insurance agents. Leonie knew them all, and, wearing her glasses, had no trouble identifying them. Pleasant greetings fired her good humour.

Near the corner of Maple and First a small group had gathered. Perhaps five or six men. The interest was a gleaming yellow and chrome touring car parked at the kerb. The back seat was swathed in a black leather raincover. The driver's seat seemed to be crammed with sticks and dials and pedals. And a very large man dressed in black trousers, grey sweater and a big smile. Leonie swallowed her smile as her internal happiness barometer fell to a new low. Him again.

'Packard,' he announced to one of the curious bystanders. '1928 Touring Car, modified. And—you'll have to pardon me.' Instead of opening a door he sidled along the front seat to the kerbside, then vaulted out on to the pavement. And, with a step or two, there he was directly in front of her.

Leonie came to a screeching halt. There *were* black clouds in those silver linings. Any fool could see that. She elevated her chin and sniffed at him.

'Good morning, Miss Marshal. Catching cold, are we?'

'I should be so lucky,' she grumbled. 'It's more likely some fatal oriental virus. Wheeleritus, probably. What are you doing here?'

'Wheeleritus? Very good.' He chuckled, a deep vibrant sound that matched his broad smile. 'Very clever.' He offered her a slight bow. 'Parking my car is what I'm doing,' he said. 'Enjoying the day. Waiting for you.'

'Very funny,' she muttered as she tried to side-step around him. With no luck. He matched her every move.

'I'll bet you're surprised to see I've got my car back so quickly.'

'Leave it on the streets and you'll find it up on jacks with everything stripped,' she snapped. 'Just because this is a small town doesn't mean we don't have our share of car thieves.' She tried another side-step. Her temper flared. 'What *is* it with you?' She stamped her foot. The pavement was one of the few in town newly repaired. Her low-heeled shoes were thin. The sole of her foot immediately complained, which only added to her ire.

'I need to talk to you,' he told her. 'Some place away from my daughter and your aunt. I thought we might have breakfast together.'

'I've had breakfast, and I'm already late for school,' she said.

'A few minutes? That isn't the type of school that has fixed periods and lectures.'

'But it *is* the sort of school that has twenty-eight students between the ages of three and six, all of whom need supervision. If you want to talk to me you'll have to come to the school.'

The argument had superseded the Packard in interest. All of the little group abandoned the car and gathered in a semi-circle around them, listening in.

'Damn,' he muttered. 'It's like trying to date your girlfriend in the middle of Harvard Stadium. Is there never a time when——? Dear lord, come on!' His right hand locked on her arm, just above the elbow, and he began to hurry her along.

'Dear lord is right,' she snapped as she tried to pull free. 'I can't walk that fast. And I am *not* your girlfriend!'

He gave her arm a little shake. 'You *might* be one day,' he chided her in a threatening voice. But he did slow down.

'I ought to call the cops,' she muttered as he steered her around the corner and across the street.

'Go ahead. Call them. I don't see a badge anywhere in sight.'

Leonie was too honest to leave it at that. 'No,' she said, sighing. 'And you won't. The depression has gotten so bad that six months ago the town council disbanded the police department.'

'And the town has no policemen at all?'

'None at all.'

'But—surely. Robbery? Crime?'

'Oh, we have all of that. The state police barracks takes care of our interests. Unfortunately they're eighteen miles away, and have five other towns under their jurisdiction. But they come when called. It averages about an hour and a half before they get here, but they come.' She looked up at him out of the corner of her eye. A disbelieving look flashed across his face. 'Maybe you don't want to locate your headquarters in Fairview? Why don't you give it a second thought?'

He pulled her to a stop and grinned down at her. 'Nice try, but not a chance. It isn't my business I'm worried about.'

'Then what?'

'That's for me to know and for you to guess,' he said. Suddenly the laughter was gone from his face, and his voice dropped deeper into the baritone scale.

'Secrets? Or are you the regional Mafia man?'

His face lit up again. He gave her arm a little tug. They were at the door of the DeMello building. The school was on the second floor. 'You're not going to believe this,' he said confidentially, 'but I'm worried about my girlfriend's safety.'

'You're right,' she returned in the same tone. 'I'm not going to believe it.' And then she bustled by him and started to climb the stairs. That irrepressible grin was back on his face, but she couldn't see it.

There were already a dozen parents in the upper hall, each with his or her darling. Leonie managed a cheery salute as she unlocked the door and stood aside. The children, from long practice, flooded into the two schoolrooms, heading for their favourite toy boxes. Their parents, from an equal amount of practice, gave satisfied sighs and disappeared down the stairs, forced to one side by the influx of the remaining parents.

'I don't know what we would do without you,' one of the departing parents told Leonie, who was standing at the door. She gave the tall, thin man an enquiring look as she rushed out.

'It must be a problem for them,' Charlie Wheeler said in an undertone.

'Half of them couldn't work if they had no place for their children, and someone to watch over them,' she returned. 'You could change all that, of course.'

'By murdering all the children? I suppose that might be the Mafia way.'

Leonie's head snapped up, prepared to fire a barrage at him. But that grin was back. 'You can laugh,' she snapped, 'but it's no laughing matter for the rest of us.'

'No, I'm sure it isn't. Now, about that talk.'

'What are you,' Leonie gasped, 'some sort of magician? Twenty-eight little children, and you want me to stop and talk? They have to be organised and led, or there'll be some sort of small riot come ten minutes from now.'

In fact the riot was already under way. Three-year-old Susan Bledsoe was sitting in the middle of the floor crying, her two hands clutching a ragged old bear. Willie Smith, four years old, was doing his best to snatch it away from her.

'You don't do things like that to little girls,' Charlie Wheeler said as he tried to separate the couple. Willie's face turned brick-red as he geared up to outcry the girl. Wheeler looked over his shoulder, appealing to Leonie. She shrugged at him, and then walked over to the music centre in the corner of the room. A crash of cymbals brought all the children to a halt.

'Morning parade,' Leonie called as the band music swelled and filled the room. All but one of the children gathered in a rough sort of formation and began to parade around the room. Knees stepped high, arms swung, eyes gleamed as they followed each other around the room. All except little Susan Bledsoe, who remained on the floor in the middle of the room, holding her bear as close as her little arms would allow.

'You want me to——?' he began.

Leonie held out a warning hand. 'When she feels like it, she'll join.'

But instead of joining the march, little Susan levered herself up on to her feet and trundled over to stand in front of Wheeler. 'Me,' she said, holding both hands—and the bear—up to him. He looked helplessly over at Leonie.

'I'm not much good with little children,' he said.

'Who would have known?' she said, chuckling. 'Pick her up and cuddle her.'

The march music came to an end. The children dropped to the floor in place, out of breath, laughing.

'All right,' Leonie called. 'Everyone into his own group.' Twenty-eight children began to mill around, dividing themselves into five, roughly equal groups by age.

'I have this problem,' Charlie Wheeler announced urgently.

'In a minute,' Leonie told him as she divided the older children into study groups, complete with colouring books. The two small groups of the youngest children gathered round her as she picked up the book she had been reading to them.

'I have this problem,' Charlie Wheeler announced again impatiently. He was holding little Susan with both hands but in a peculiar fashion, away from his body. And at that moment Mary Parker, Leonie's part-time assistant, came bustling in. Little Susan stretched out her hands and squealed. Mary gave one look at the embarrassed male and collected the baby with care.

'It happens on occasion,' she told Wheeler. 'Susan is our youngest, and when she gets excited——' The two of them, Mary and the baby, disappeared down the hall.

Wheeler walked over and stood behind Leonie. 'You knew that all the time,' he muttered. 'And enjoyed it.'

'Children are children,' she answered, and then returned to her story.

'Damn.'

'No swearing in front of the children!'

'I'd like to——'

'Break my neck?'

'Kiss you,' he said. She was sitting on the floor, part of the circle of children. He picked her up as if she were one of those children, cuddled her up against himself, and did just what he had threatened. With vigour and enthusiasm and a great deal of experience. The children, watching avidly, yelled their approval and clapped their hands.

'Stop that!' she hissed at him as he set her down on her feet. 'This is not a peep show. You set a bad example for the children!' She tugged at her skirt and smoothed down her blouse, but could not cool the storm raging inside her.

'You liked it,' he said. 'You're a patsy for a quick kiss. Besides, I'll bet half these kids never see real affection displayed at home. We're setting a *good* example for the dear little tykes.'

She was watching him carefully as he spoke. There was more than a little disdain on his face.

'It's true, isn't it?' she demanded to know. 'You really *don't* like children! No wonder your daughter is such a——'

'Such a tough little kid? No, I owe that to her mother's tender concern. She used to coach our daughter into believing that her father was a no-good.'

'Well, I didn't appreciate it at all,' Leonie said as she dropped back into a yoga position on the floor and thumbed through her book to see where she had left off. 'Oh, by the way, where *is* your daughter?'

'In her bed when I left,' he said.

'Not when *I* left. I thought you might have taken her with you.'

'Story,' one of the children in the group called. Two others joined her. Leonie found the right page.

'Not at the house?' he asked.

'Not at the house,' she confirmed.

'Damn!'

'Mr Wheeler, *please*. No swearing.'

He glared down at her for a moment, then turned on his heel and stomped off.

'Damn,' said the angelic little blonde nestling up to Leonie's knee.

'We don't say that,' Leonie said icily. 'Now, where were we?'

By five o'clock the last of the parents had come, the last of the children had gone. There was none of the usual laughter. During the early part of the afternoon, when all the children were napping, Leonie had managed to reach each of the twenty-eight families by telephone and explain the problem.

'Yes,' she'd promised each of them. 'We'll keep open until the last day, and I'll refund that part of the tuition which the school didn't earn.'

There had been shock, anger, tears. Six of the families, unable to find any other solution to the problem, had begged Leonie to take their children into her own home until they could find some other solution.

'I'm sorry, but I can't,' Leonie had said, half crying. 'I need to find a job myself. No, the cows can't support me. They have to go too.'

And so there were tears in her own eyes as she made one more last tour of the classrooms, and went out into the hall just as more footsteps came thundering up the stairs. Charlie Wheeler—and, tagging along behind him belligerently, his daughter Cecilia. The child was dragging her heels, but was being towed along by her father.

'I was just about to lock up,' Leonie said. Actually, her key was already in the lock.

'We'll need a few minutes. I *told* you I needed to talk to you. Now the need is greater.' He opened the door and pushed his daughter through into the classroom. Leonie followed hesitantly. The Wheelers looked like two matching volcanoes, about to erupt. They stood in the middle of the room, glaring at the world.

'I don't think I want to hear what's wrong,' Leonie half whispered.

'You'll listen,' he said, at a level just below hurricane strength. His daughter shrank away from him.

Oil on troubled waters, Leonie told herself. Casual conversation. Something light and frothy? 'I'm glad you found your daughter.'

It wasn't frothy enough. 'She has a name: Cecilia. I'm glad I found her too!'

'Where was she?'

'Among other places, out in your pasture.'

'I——' Is that my fault? Leonie asked herself. 'You didn't hire us to baby-sit for you,' she said finally. 'I don't think I could have, what with all the other troubles I have.'

'Ask me what she was doing in your barn.'

'What is this, some sort of guessing game?'

'Ask.'

'OK. What was she doing in my barn? Playing in the hay loft?'

'You are about as naïve as they come,' he grumbled. 'Maybe that's why I like you so much.'

'Maybe that's why'—— Something caught in Leonie's throat. 'Like you so much'? He's talking about me? The *me* that he's doing his best to ruin? Has already ruined, for that matter. So I'm naïve. I admit that. Even Jeff said that. Even Aunt Agnes said that. And I said, Who, me? Lord, what's going on here?

'Look at this.' He pulled something out of the paper bag he was carrying. Something metallic. Leonie focused. It was easy to identify. A metal spur. One of a pair her grandfather had used. It was old and tired and rusty, and there was something black on the rowel. She snatched it out of his hand and ran her finger across the rowel.

'Blood?' There was a question behind the question. Her voice quavered.

'Blood,' he confirmed.

'What——?' And then it came to her. 'Where's Dandy?'

'Out in the pasture. He's down and can't get up. I don't know enough about horses to see why. You'd better come.'

'I—yes. I'll follow you out in my car. What——?'

'Cecilia, tell the lady.'

The girl managed to work her hand loose and retreated to the corner of the library table. Her father glared at her.

'I wanted a ride,' the child said. 'He wouldn't go. In all the cowboy movies they——' She stopped and knuckled her eyes. 'And then when he did go, out in the middle of the pasture he stumbled and threw me right over his head. Why don't nobody care about *me* gettin' hurt, 'stead of an old, worn-out horse?'

'You were hurt?'

'Aunt Agnes looked her over,' he said. 'A few scratches and bruises, nothing more. Let's go.'

'Just another minute,' Leonie said. Dandy was down and couldn't get up? What's happening to my world? she asked herself. She rubbed one hand over her forehead. A migraine was developing. I love that old horse, she thought. As she thought she dialled.

'Yes, I can spare a few minutes,' Mr Alfast, the town veterinarian said. 'I'll meet you at the farm.'

'Now we'll go.' Leonie looked down at the little girl, still cowering in the corner by the table. Cowering, but with a defiant look on her face, her teeth slightly bared, prepared to bite the world.

And me too, Leonie told herself as she placed herself as far from the child as she could get. It was a mutual dislike, obviously. The girl snarled like a fox with one leg caught in a trap.

'We'll go in my car,' he announced as they crossed the street.

'What, and leave my——?'

'I don't trust your driving,' he said. 'Even with your glasses I don't trust your driving. I'll send some one over to pick up your car.'

'Well, la-di-da,' Leonie muttered.

'What?'

'Nothing. I said—it's a lovely car,' she lied. He glared at her, as if all the syllables hadn't come out quite right.

It was a wide car, with plenty of room in the front seat for all three of them. Cecilia did her best to sit in the middle without touching either one of them. The leather upholstery was aromatic. Leonie was unable to identify the smell, but it was nice. It was a manual drive, of course, with a couple of extra levers she could not name.

The engine purred. 'Sounds nice,' she complimented him.

He looked as if he was astonished at the compliment. 'Modified,' he said. 'Sixteen cylinders.' He did something with the gear lever. They moved out into traffic as if gliding on ice. There was considerable assistance, of course. Drivers coming and going were so surprised at the magnificence of the car that they all stopped to observe, leaving him plenty of room to slip into the traffic flow.

'That doesn't hurt your ego, does it?' Leonie queried.

He was not a man to appreciate sarcasm. He took his eyes off the traffic to glare at her. 'What?'

Time to shut up, Leonie told herself. Damn well past time. She worked up a tentative smile, but he wasn't appeased. Cecilia broke into the conversation.

'She said the car's nice to go.'

'Oh?' Said suspiciously, as if he doubted everything except the punctuation.

'Watch where you're driving, please.' Leonie sniffed at him and turned to watch the scenery go by. I'm doing a lot of that, aren't I? she asked herself. Sniffing at him. Hauteur. The royal sniff. He has only two responses. Either he glares at me or he kisses me. And I wish I could understand why, or know which response I preferred! And his daughter?

Back on Main Street he picked up speed. The wind came over the curved windscreen and eddied around in the open interior. Leonie reached into her bag for a scarf, and used it to bind her heavy hair in place. Cecilia squirmed in her seat, shifting slightly closer to her father. The movement reminded Leonie of their mission.

Dandy. What could have happened to Dandy? Of course, twenty-five-year-old horses were not exactly equipped for racing. Not any more. There had been a time when Dandy could run with the best of them in the neighbourhood quarter-horse races. A long time ago when Leonie was a little girl.

So immersed was she in her dreams that she hardly noticed where they were until Charlie Wheeler put his foot on the brakes to slow them down, and then swung the big, heavy car off the road and into the driveway by the house. Another car already stood in the drive.

'Mr Alfast is already here,' Leonie said as the Packard came to a halt just behind the two-year-old Lincoln Continental.

'Vets must live high on the hog,' Wheeler said as he helped both of his passengers out. There was a taste of sarcasm in his voice.

'We live in the country,' Leonie snapped. 'Veterinarians are worth their weight in gold, and——'

The back door creaked open and Aunt Agnes and the vet both came out. The vet was a roly-poly man, some five feet seven, and sixty years old. He possessed a smile that gleamed in the fading sun almost as much as did his completely bald pate.

'I've just this minute arrived,' he announced. 'It's getting dark. We'd better hurry.' And then, belying his words, he stopped. 'It's not my line of work, Leonie,' he said, 'but you're looking a sight more peaked than you ought to be.'

'I—just have a lot of troubles——' Leonie muttered.

'Like the daughter of Job,' Aunt Agnes interrupted.

'Let's get to Dandy,' Leonie said. 'Once he's settled things will be better. Where is he—Mr Wheeler?'

The tall, thin man at her side winced. 'Charlie,' he said. 'Charlie.' He ran a big hand nervously through his hair. 'The horse is down at the far north corner of the pasture.'

'Then we'll use the tractor,' Leonie decided. 'Can't expect Mr Alfast to walk all that far. Room for three.'

'Cecilia, you stay here with Aunt Agnes,' Charlie ordered.

'I ought to go,' the girl said.

'No. There's no need for that,' Leonie told her. 'What's done is done. There's no use crying over spilt milk.'

The child's father looked down at Leonie as if she had lost her mind. He started to say something, then wheeled and headed off to the barn. The vet trailed along behind him, his heavy bag bouncing off his thighs.

The tractor was a heavy four-wheel Zodiac, old enough to have been ploughing the farm before Leonie was born. But it had been kept in good condition. The ignition caught immediately, and barely a moment later the heavy diesel engine burst into song. The two men squeezed into the bench seat, and Leonie balanced herself in the bucket seat and guided them gently out of the barn and into the pasture.

The sun had already begun to flirt with the tops of the Berkshires. The tractor possessed a single spotlight. Leonie flashed it on. The pasture was flush with autumn grass, but the going was a little rough. There were ridges and hollows and ruts, all hidden by that lush grass.

The trip across the pasture took ten minutes, and they came upon the horse suddenly. Dandy was lying head-down in a small ditch. His head came up when the noise of the tractor invaded his mind. Leonie braked to a stop, but chubby Mr Alfast was on the ground first.

Leonie manoeuvred the light stanchion so that the accident scene was well-lit, and then followed. The vet was leaning over the horse, making soothing noises as his hands traced the two forelegs. Charlie Wheeler, acting as if he were a mind-reader, came up behind Leonie and put his arms around her. She leaned back into the warmth of him, knowing what was going to be said before a word was uttered. The three of them stood there as the sun set, a trio of statues in the huge darkness of the pasture. And then the veterinarian climbed up out of the ditch.

'I'm sorry, Leonie,' the doctor said gruffly. 'He must have been moving at some speed beyond his control when he put both legs into the ditch. They're both broken!'

There was no need to explain. Leonie moaned as she slipped out of Charlie's comforting arms and slid down into the ditch beside the horse. Dandy managed to lift his head slightly. 'Oh, love,' she muttered as she tried to cuddle his heavy head against her. The horse whinnied. For a moment they formed another silhouette, the girl and her horse. And then the horse groaned as his head fell back on to the ground.

Weary beyond belief, Leonie patted the neck of her favourite animal, and then climbed back out of the ditch. Charlie Wheeler held out one hand and drew her up on to level ground. She went to his arms again, this time slowly, and faltering.

'There's no hope,' the vet said. 'He's too old to cure. We'll have to put him down.'

'Yes,' she said, sighing. 'But I—I can't do it. Could you——?'

'Of course,' the vet said. 'Why don't you walk back to the house? I'll bring the tractor back when I'm finished.'

Leonie hesitated for one more look down at the horse, and then turned towards the house, whose lights were gleaming in the twilight across the pasture. She took one step in that direction, paused, and then another. It was hard walking. The pasture was relatively flat, but it felt as if she was walking uphill. There was a pain in her heart. And then Charlie Wheeler was at her side.

His arm came around her. For a moment she stopped in that comforting warmth, and when she started walking again he stayed with her, one arm around her shoulders, the other holding her hand. The shared warmth was a comfort. She lifted her feet higher. It was like walking on the beach out into the incoming tide, with the waves pulsing at her, slowing her down, chilling her legs.

They were halfway across the field when they heard the sharp crack of the revolver. Leonie stopped, turned towards Charles, and clung to him. And now the tears came—roiling, gushing tears.

'Dandy and I—for a long time,' she managed between the tears. 'I know he's old, but I never thought—— Lord, why is all this happening to me? Why now, all at once?'

'Only God knows,' he said. His lips were almost at her ear. With a gentleness Leonie had never known before, he kissed her. She broke away from him as her mind went back into gear.

My school is lost, my horse is dead, my dairy has got to go. Job never had it so tough. And her temper rose. They were a short distance from the house, and the tractor was roaring up behind them. It was just the time, the only time, when she could speak to him privately.

'Mr Wheeler,' she said harshly, 'enough is enough. You've already ruined all the ways I have to make a living, and your daughter has managed to destroy the animal closest to my heart. I want the pair of you to pack up and get out of my house—and my life.'

He put a huge hand on each of her shoulders and turned her so that the beam from the approaching tractor illuminated her face. There was not a glimmer of humour in *his* face; two tears were running down hers.

'You have good reason to complain,' he admitted, 'but I can't do it. There's just no place else to live in this town. I have a written contract with your aunt Agnes for thirty days of lodgings. I don't intend to leave before then.'

'Damn you,' she muttered under her breath. 'I hope you go bankrupt and catch a bad case of shingles!'

'Thanks a lot,' he growled, and stalked off towards the house.

CHAPTER FIVE

ON SATURDAY morning at nine, three weeks later, Leonie was at the table, fully dressed, when Aunt Agnes, wearing an old grey robe and shabby slippers, came out to the kitchen. 'I can't get accustomed to this,' the older lady said, laughing. 'Here you are just sitting.'

'And on my second cup of coffee,' Leonie said, trying to add a little humour to the situation. 'My bones aren't really prepared for this layabout life.'

'It's good for you,' Aunt Agnes said as she busied herself about the coffee-pot. 'You were so haggard, love. So worn out. I can't help but think it's all for the better.'

'Maybe,' Leonie replied. 'Closing the playschool was a relief of sorts. There were just too many kids involved. And too many parents who knew better than I about running things.'

'And the dairy auction yesterday—that'll help too.'

'Yes, I suppose so, but I wish I were sure we'd be able to eat regularly.'

'You mustn't forget, Leonie, I still have money in my bank account.'

'I won't forget, Aunt Agnes, but I've no intention of dipping into your funds.'

'And why not, may I ask? You've been supporting me for the past six years. I haven't contributed a thing in all that time.'

'What *are* you talking about?' Leonie came up out of her chair and hugged the old lady. 'I was so lonely before you came to live with me—you've contributed a very great deal, my dear. The books were thoroughly screwed

75

up, too. You were just what I needed. A retired maths teacher! Here. Sit down while I whip you up a couple of eggs. Thank the Lord we still have the chickens.'

She ushered Aunt Agnes back to the table and then returned to the stove. In a moment she was busy with eggs and country sausages and toast.

'And we have each other,' she said as she carried a loaded plate to the table.

'And Charlie,' her aunt added. 'I won't say, And Cecilia. She's around the house but not exactly in it these past weeks.'

'I could have gone all day without your mentioning Charlie Wheeler,' Leonie murmured as she sat down to her coffee-mug. Charlie Wheeler. They lived in a big house, but that man was too big to be ignored. She couldn't blot him out of her mind even when she shut her bedroom door behind her. Charlie Wheeler...she mused. When he isn't in the house he seems to haunt it. And what makes things worse is I can't afford to cut off his bed-and-breakfast lease. It's the only money we have coming into the house now! I'd just love to——

'He loaned us the money to pay off the school tuition debts, didn't he?'

'Yes, and the supply account as well. Damn it!' And that's another reason why I don't like him, she told herself. He made the offer to pay off the entire bill just at the time I couldn't refuse it. I *hate* to be obligated to that—man.

'As soon as we get the cheque from the auction house, he's the first one I'd want you to pay off, Aunt Agnes.'

'Ah. I wouldn't want to stick my nose into your problems, love, but I'm sure he's in no hurry to be paid back. And he's paying us something for looking after Cecilia in after-school hours.'

'Damn!'

'It's not a loan. The child needs looking after.'

'Yes, I'm sure she does. But she hasn't said a word to me for weeks. How can I look after her if I haven't a clue what she's all about?'

'Nor I. She goes off to school, comes home, throws her books in her bedroom, and then disappears. Ever since Dandy——'

'Please, Aunt Agnes, I don't want to talk about that.'

'No, I don't suppose you do,' the old lady said compassionately.

There was a moment or two of silence.

'And what do you plan for today?'

Leonie shook her head. 'I'm not sure, but I'm considering cleaning out the barn. When they said auction *everything* off I hadn't expected that was just what they meant: the cows, the stalls, the equipment, even the hay and feed I had stored. And that old horse-drawn harrow that grandfather last used, as well as the thirty-year-old tractor. Everything!'

'I suppose that's for the best. Do you know how well we did?'

'No. The auction house will send you a summary pretty soon. I can't imagine who would want all that—junk.'

'Leonie! Your grandfather highly appreciated all that "junk".'

'Yes, I suppose he did. He was a dear old man. I miss him.'

Leonie pushed her chair back and carried her coffee-mug over to the sink.

'And brush your hair,' Aunt Agnes said.

'To clean the barn I should brush my hair?'

'You never know whom you might meet, love. You have lovely hair. But that dress you're wearing is about ready for the rag bag.'

'So am I,' Leonie murmured. But living with Aunt
Agnes had taught her something. If brushing my hair
makes Aunt Agnes feel better, well, what the hey? she
thought. So she went back to her bedroom to do just
that. And at the same time she gave some consideration
to her dress. Which did not, she thought, even seem good
enough for the rag bag. And so into a pair of relatively
decent jeans and a flannel blouse, suitable for barn-
cleaning, but just the tiniest bit too tight around the
bosom.

Aunt Agnes, only halfway through her breakfast,
smiled at the *new* Leonie Marshal and tipped her a salute
as the girl went out of the back door.

Leonie sauntered down the path that led to the barn.
The sun was up, but not too warm. There were white
clouds in the sky, floating eastwards on the long trip to
rain down on Boston, she feverishly hoped. For some
reason she had developed a loathing for politicians and
bureaucrats. Aunt Agnes, who handled all the money
and accounts, had told her that the last two milk subsidy
cheques were six weeks overdue and had left them very
short of cash at a critical time. And if it hadn't been for
the loan from Charlie Wheeler—— Damn that man!
Why does he have to be so nice just when I work up a
good hate? she asked herself.

Her dog, Tighe, was stretched out on the stone path,
just at the back corner of the house. Hearing her footsteps, he came slowly up on four feet, wagged his tail a
time or two, and nudged his head towards her. Leonie
leaned down to pat the ancient head. 'You miss Dandy,
don't you?' she offered. Almost as if he understood the
language, the dog licked her hand. 'I guess we all
do,' Leonie murmured. Tighe sat down to await
further instructions.

Leonie took a deep breath. Both the shoe factories in Fairview had shut down months ago. The unemployment figures had climbed astronomically; the air pollution had decreased in the same proportion.

'It's hard to know,' Leonie told her dog, 'whether it's better to breathe easier or eat more regularly.'

Tighe offered one wag of his tail. The depression had not yet affected *his* food supply. And at that moment there came a clatter from the barn, and a profusion of four-letter words from an aggravated male voice. Leonie turned to look down the hill.

The old barn had been kept up, far better than the house itself. Its red sides and brown doors glistened in the autumn sun. The game-cock weather vane swung idly between north and north-west. All the doors were open. Somebody's mucking the place out? she asked herself. She gave Tighe another scratch behind the ears and started down the path. The closer she came, the noisier the barn sounded. Leonie made her way around the loading platform and stepped from daylight into darkness.

'What's going on in here?' she demanded. Two of the shadows moved in her direction. She pushed her glasses up on her nose. The Clarrigan brothers, both high-school seniors, stripped to the waist and sweating profusely, came forward. They lived four houses down the street.

'Well,' the older brother said, 'we was offered this job, and——'

'I hired them.' The third shadow came closer. Charlie Wheeler, also stripped to the waist. Leonie backed off a step or two, to where the sun lit the doorway. Wheeler waved the two young men back to work, and stepped out to join her.

'I thought things needed cleaning,' Wheeler said, as he loomed over her. Leonie had trouble swallowing.

Living in the country, she had seen her share and more of stripped-down males. But none of them had affected her as much as this one. From wide shoulder to narrow waist the V-shape of his torso was enough to set her mind afire. During the past three weeks of eating at the Marshal table he had put on considerable weight, practically all of it muscle. There was a long scar down his right side, from rib to waistline. An old scar. It gleamed white against the tan of his skin.

His black hair had been trimmed to a military cut. And his teeth gleamed at her. 'The better to eat you with', she thought, dazed. It was hard to hate a man who had all that going for him!

'Don't you think so?' he asked. Leonie snapped back to attention. He had said something else—several somethings else, and she had missed it all.

Rather than appear like a total idiot, she gathered up a little smile. 'Of course,' she said.

'Good,' he replied. 'I like a woman who makes up her mind. The boys will finish up the rough work in about an hour. I'll have the carpenter come in Monday.'

'I—seem to have lost track,' she said, shaking her head. 'All this work on the barn?'

'Very necessary,' he said. 'Your aunt and I have agreed on a six-month extension on our bed-and-breakfast contract. And my car——'

'Six months? Your car?' Cold chills ran up and down her spine. Could she maintain her distance from him for six months? Why didn't Aunt Agnes tell me? she wondered.

'Yes. I can't leave it parked outside forever. It's an expensive vehicle, and——'

'And you'll be here six months more?'

'Just so.'

He might have said more, but at that moment the two young men came over. 'All finished,' the older reported. 'We'll come over with our truck and cart the junk out to the dump.'

'Thanks a lot, boys. I left your pay in the house with Aunt Agnes. She's evidently the paymaster around here.'

The two of them went out, ragging each other, running up the hill. Tighe, still holding position at the corner of the house, managed a magnificent bark. The two runners made a wide sweep around the dog's claim, and went slamming into the house.

And you'll be here six months more, Leonie thought as she turned back towards Charlie Wheeler. Six months more? She wasn't quite sure whether she was glad or not, but in the three weeks since Dandy was put down her temper had cooled and——

'Help me,' he interrupted. She blinked her eyes into focus. His back was turned towards her, and there was a towel in his hands. He deposited it into her hands and bent over slightly.

'W-what?' she stammered.

'Dry,' he commanded. There was a trace of a chuckle in his voice as he looked back at her over his shoulder. 'I'm dripping and I can't do my back.'

'I—yes, I can see that,' she murmured. She shook out the towel and began to rub his shoulders. Her hand slipped off the towel for just a second and touched the hard bronze flesh. An electric shock ran up her spine. She breathed heavily, although the task was slight.

'Harder,' he commanded.

She complied. I'm *touching* him, she told herself. I haven't touched a man since Jeff. A long time ago. And that was a terrible mistake. But while her mind kept saying, Stop, her heart kept saying, Go. Despite all her little hatreds—and that, she told herself, is what the struggle is all about, isn't it? Do I hate him? She rubbed harder.

'That's good,' he commented.

Yes, that is, she thought. He's the sort of man you have to either love or hate. There doesn't seem to be any other choice. Do I hate him? No? Then——

'Oh, lord,' she gasped. The towel slipped from her hands and crumpled itself up on the newly cleaned floor. He straightened. Leonie, fully conscious of what she was doing, backed away. I *have* to hate him, she told herself. I couldn't possibly——

'I guess that's enough,' he said. That amiable grin was back. 'And I do thank you.'

'Y-yes,' she stuttered. 'I—that's enough. You ought to go in and take a shower. You shouldn't have done all this.' She waved one hand vaguely at the sparkling interior of the barn. 'You'll catch a chill.'

'Had to do it,' he returned. 'I couldn't think of storing my classic car in a dirty barn. By the way, how much rent do you propose to charge for the parking space?'

'Rent? I—I haven't any idea. You'll have to take that up with Aunt Agnes.'

There, she told herself. I've done it again. If I were being honest I would have said, None at all. But I need all the money I can get, and haven't the nerve to set a price. What's wrong with me? I've never been so confused in all my days. Or at least I don't think I have!

'But for the price of cleaning up the barn?'

'I—I can't charge you for that. I suppose I really owe you.'

'That's what I like to hear. A businesslike approach to the whole affair, right?'

'Er—right.'

'But I can't charge you too much.'

I'm glad, she thought. As of the moment the Marshal family is flat broke, but I can't tell *him* that! 'What are you doing?'

While she dithered he had walked across the small space that separated them. 'Collecting my pay,' he said.

'But I——'

And again he interrupted. His arms came around her and pillowed her against his chest. She struggled for a nano-second, and then relaxed. He held her steady for a moment or two, and then used a finger to tilt her chin up.

Don't look, she told herself. Close your eyes! She did. His warm lips came down on hers. Soft, moist and sweet. How stupid can you get? she berated herself. You have to close your eyes because he's kissing you? Aren't there any women who can kiss with their eyes open? Luckily her curiosity was overwhelmed by the pleasure of it all, and she gave herself up to the moment.

'And that wasn't half bad,' he commented as he set her gently aside. 'Now I can get at my business.'

'It's Saturday,' she said. He grinned at her. She had been unable to get that little forlorn touch out of her voice. 'Nobody works on Saturday.'

'A lot you know,' he returned. 'My planning people are due in today. By the way, would you like to sell the furniture you had in the school?'

'Sell? It wasn't worth moving, and——'

'My people need some immediate places to sit and work,' he said.

Can't you ever let me finish a sentence? she thought.

'How much would you want for the lot?'

'I—I don't know.' Four weeks ago I was an independent business woman, with facts and figures in my head, she thought. Now I can't even put a price on the time of day. I just don't know what to say.

'OK. I understand. I have to see Aunt Agnes about that.' He chucked her under the chin, leaned over and planted a soft kiss on her forehead, and walked out of the barn whistling.

So he's not perfect, she told herself. He can't whistle worth a darn. And then another thought. How in the world were all those adult planners of his going to sit at those tiny children's desks the school had owned? There wasn't any answer.

Somewhat dazed, Leonie walked out on to the loading platform and sat down, tucking her knees up under her chin. Her ever-faithful dog Tighe was giving Charlie Wheeler a royal welcome as the man went by. And what do you suppose all that means? she asked herself. Male-to-male rapport, or real affection? Or treason?

The sun was flooding the barn by this time, warming her. She stared up at the house until he went in, and then continued to stare, as if his shadow were still in sight. Her fingers played with her heavy russet hair. 'Brush your hair', Aunt Agnes said. And so I did. Did dear, faithful Aunt Agnes know that Charlie Wheeler was out in the barn? she asked herself. Can it be that there's a little conspiracy going on here? Unconsciously her fingers busied themselves with her fall of hair, establishing a parting and beginning to braid. And if there were, would I be angry?

The voice at her elbow startled her. 'You have lovely hair,' Cecilia said. Leonie looked over her shoulder. The girl was standing just behind her, legs parted slightly, looking her usually chunky self.

'Thank you,' Leonie said. It's time to welcome both of them, she told herself. 'Care to sit for a while?'

The girl scrambled down into a yoga position. She was simply dressed—a pair of worn blue denims, a yellow blouse, worn shoes with no socks.

'You're not cold?'

The girl looked at her strangely. 'You're worried about me being cold? You hate me, don't you?'

For the second time in one day the Wheeler family had managed to surprise Leonie Marshal. 'Hate? I don't think so.'

'But you don't like me.'

'I wouldn't say that either. I haven't really come to a conclusion.'

'I don't mind if you hate me. My dad hates me. And everybody at that school hates me too. The kids *and* the teachers! I might as well be back in your playschool.'

Whoa up here, Leonie thought. Everybody hates her? The poor kid! But it *could* be true. Her father seldom speaks to her at the house nowadays. And any new kid in a schoolroom has a hard time of it until she establishes herself in the pecking order.

'You hate me because of Dandy. You loved that horse, didn't you?' It was an accusation, as if Leonie were to blame for loving a horse—that 'old, worn-out horse'.

'I think you've got that mixed up,' Leonie said. 'Yes, I loved that horse. He and I grew up together. And yes, I was angry when he—died. But there's a great deal of difference between anger and hatred.'

The girl cocked her head and stared at Leonie's face. 'I don't understand.'

'Anger is a flare-up of emotion,' Leonie told her. 'It comes and goes. Hatred is something very much worse, and lasts a long time. I was angry with you about Dandy. You showed poor judgement in what you did. But then, you're not an adult, and I could hardly judge you by adult standards. I've put Dandy away in my memories. And I don't hate you.'

'If I was you I would hate me.'

'But you're not me and I don't. Now, why do you think your dad hates you?'

'Because he never talks to me no more. Because he knows I wanted to stay with my mom. I never wanted to come with him.'

'So why did you?'

'Because—because.'

Leonie looked closely. The adamant Cecilia was as close to crying as could be. The moisture was already clouding her eyes.

'Because why?'

The girl vaulted to her feet. Her hands were extended stiffly down her sides, the fingers of both hands clenched so tightly that the circulation was cut off. 'Damn you,' she muttered. Her hands came up between them, like a boxer waiting for the bell. Her clenched fists threatened, and then fell away as the child's whole frame slumped. 'Because my mom didn't want me either,' she said, gasping!

Leonie uncoiled and stood up. The child stared at her. Tears were running down the girl's cheeks. There seemed to be only one thing to do. Leonie opened her arms, and Cecilia walked into them. And the tears ran. Not in buckets, just in a small, steady stream, accompanied by sobs that would tear your heart out. 'Nobody loves me,' the child wailed, and then all the dams broke.

Leonie pulled her tough little body close, and made soothing noises—comfort without words—until gradually the tears slacked off.

'There now,' Leonie coaxed. 'Better?'

The girl backed off a step or two, knuckled at her eyes, and nodded.

'I didn't mean to cry all over your blouse.'

'Think nothing of it,' Leonie teased. 'I have another one in my closet somewhere. C'mon. Let's go get something to eat.'

Cecilia's eyes sparkled through the damp. The child fished in her pockets for the second-dirtiest handkerchief in all of Massachusetts and wiped her cheeks and nose.

'I could use a friend more than a meal,' Cecilia said mournfully.

'I don't see why you couldn't have both,' Leonie returned. 'Come on.' And taking the girl's hand in hers she went down the ramp and up the path. Tighe, still lying in the sun, came to his four wobbly feet and wagged his tail.

'See,' Leonie said. 'That makes two.'

Charlie Wheeler came back to the old farmhouse at noon.

'We would have waited for you,' Leonie said, 'but the food was getting cold.'

He made a big production out of looking at his wristwatch. 'Yes, I see. I'm five minutes late for lunch and a dollar short, but *you* can't wait.'

'That's about the way of it,' his daughter said. He looked over at her, but she ducked her head and stuffed another forkful of spaghetti into her mouth.

Leonie watched the pair of them. For the first time in weeks they were smiling at each other. Secretly she congratulated herself, and then threw in a reprimand. There's no real reason to think that something *you* did brought about this change, she told herself. But then, who can tell?

He came over to the table and stood over Leonie's shoulder. 'Spaghetti?'

'As you see.'

'I hate canned spaghetti.'

'So I've been told. This is home-made. Your daughter made it.'

'I——'

A-ha! Leonie told herself. *Gotcha*! For the first time in the several weeks she had known him, Charlie Wheeler had been caught off guard. Her smile became a grin. The expression on his face told of embarrassment.

'Why, of course,' he added. 'The Wheelers are capable of almost anything.'

'Is that a compliment, Dad?' The girl beamed. It looked as if someone had turned on a powerful light within her. Her smile was expanded a thousandfold.

Look at that, Leonie told herself. She looks as if she's a child again, happy with the world. Leonie leaned over and tapped her on the shoulder. Cecilia delayed a moment, and then turned to look.

'And that,' Leonie said, 'makes three.'

Cecilia looked puzzled. Tighe wandered in at that moment, came over to the girl, and rested his old head on her knee. 'Oh,' Cecilia said. 'Like that? One, two, three?'

'Like that,' Leonie said. 'Sit you down, Mr Wheeler, and have a dish of the finest spaghetti in the county.'

He pulled out a chair, but hesitated to sit down. 'Somehow I have the feeling that you people are talking some language that's way above my head. Who's going to translate?'

'Women's talk,' his daughter advised him. 'You'd never understand.'

'Well, thank you very much,' he said, but there was a touch of humour in his remark. 'Do I understand that you've joined the female society? Where's the third witch, by the way?'

'Aunt Agnes?'

'Who else?'

'Eat your spaghetti,' Leonie said as she brought him a plate piled high from the kettle on the stove. 'This is Saturday afternoon. The Quilting Society meets every Saturday afternoon.'

'Do you say so? And how long has this been going on?'

'I'm not sure. Fifty years—something like that.'

'Ah. Most of these societies turn out to be gabfests. When is the last time they actually produced a quilt?'

'Eat, smart alec.'

He stuck his fork into the meal and twirled it like an expert. 'How long?' he challenged.

'I don't know, do I?' Leonie twirled her own fork, and did miserably at it. 'I remember they made a quilt for me. And before you make any wise remarks, it was to celebrate my birth!'

'And how long ago might that be?'

'Is that what all this conversation's about? You want to know how old I am? I'm twenty-seven. And how old are you?'

'See my white hair,' he returned. Leonie looked carefully. There wasn't a white strand to be seen. She told him so.

'Ah. My barber takes care of it,' he said, chuckling. 'I'm somewhere around thirty-five.' He took another swallow, and almost choked on one of the tiny meatballs that Cecilia had so carefully rolled. And would you look at that self-satisfied look he's wearing? Leonie thought. I don't know whether he's proud that he's so old, or glad that I'm so young.

'So what did you do this morning, Dad?'

'I went down to the office,' he said. 'Several of our new people have arrived and settled in. The corporation will be up and running by this time next week. We found an old warehouse that we'll use for central storage. Vegetables and canned goods, mainly.'

'And that's all you did?'

'Oh, no. I went over to the YMCA for a swim, and then a little old codger who looked to be about seventy-five whipped my—er—whipped me *bodaciously* at handball.'

'Those people around these parts who live long enough are very tough people,' Leonie told him. 'So, in a few weeks you'll let the good times roll?'

'Hey, this is only the beginning. First we have to get the local store up to speed, and then we'll start looking around the county for places where we can establish other stores.'

'Then I suppose you'll be looking for your own house to live in pretty soon.'

His head came up as if he sniffed trouble. 'Not soon,' he said hurriedly. 'Not soon. It'll be some time. Don't you think so, baby?'

'I'm not a baby,' Cecilia retorted. And then she put her fork down alongside her empty plate. 'And I like it here. I think we'll be here for a long time, won't we?'

'Well, this *is* a change,' he said. He studied his daughter as if he hadn't quite seen her before. Then he nodded his head as if the pair of them were sharing some secret of their own. 'Yes, we'll be here some time, I guess. There are lots of important things to get settled. I can't spend too much time worrying about living quarters.'

And I'm glad of that, Leonie thought, jolted back to reality. Lord knows, he's my only source of income these days. If Aunt Agnes weren't such a clever manager of figures we'd both be on our way to the poorhouse by now. Or is it true that poorhouses have all been long since closed?

'How about,' Charlie Wheeler said as he wiped his lips on the paper napkin, 'if I take my two women out for a ride in the Packard? I'm sure there's plenty to see around here.'

So why does a simple invitation like that make me squirm in my seat? Leonie asked. It isn't as if it were a date, not with his daughter along.

'I don't think I have the time,' Cecilia said. 'I've a load of homework to do. You two go along without me.'

Leonie felt a sudden chill run up her spine. An afternoon drive for three was ever so much different from a drive for two!

'If you say so,' her father said. 'Although I've never known you to be all *that* interested in homework.'

'I'm reformed,' Cecilia announced proudly. 'I'm a born-again student.'

'Yes,' her father said. 'And I'm an elder of the church, C'mon, Leonie. Let's get out in the fresh air. Get your hat.'

'I seldom wear hats,' she murmured. And never take commands from men! she added silently. He really ought to make Cecilia come with us. The fresh air will do the child good. And nobody should be locked into homework on weekends! Never the less she got up from the table and made for the bathroom. She knew a thing or two about taking long rides in open cars.

His Packard touring car was parked in the drive outside the back door. When Leonie came out he was busy with his polishing cloth, brushing a few grains of dust off the chrome. She closed the back door quietly behind her and watched.

Jealousy, she told herself. That's what's aching me. If I were in love with the man, how would I feel coming in second-best behind a seventy-year-old automobile? Obviously he loves his car far more than he could love any run-of-the-mill woman. Luckily I'm not in love with him, damn it!

He looked up and saw her—and laughed as if she and his car were all the requirements he needed for a perfect day. He came around and opened the door for her. She needed a little help reaching up to the running board, but after that the spacious front seat was no trouble at all.

He held the door until she was seated, then closed it carefully. No slamming doors. Leonie checked one more item off her list of things that one certainly never did. Not with an antique car.

'Ready?'

'Ready,' she murmured.

'Your seatbelt,' he challenged.

'I didn't know antique cars had seatbelts.'

'Well, this one does. It's an added safety feature.'

'But I can't reach it,' she complained meekly. 'You'll——'

He required no coaching. Somehow he was almost on top of her as he found both connectors for the belt. 'They are a little clumsy,' he said almost in her ear.

She was paying little or no attention. One of his forearms had found lodgement on her breast, and despite her heavy sweater and leather jacket was exciting more feelings than she had felt in many a year. When the two metal clamps clicked into place she felt a little bereft.

'Sorry about that,' he said, laughing.

Yeah, sure, she thought. Me too. It was extremely difficult not to let her enjoyment show. 'You're a lousy poker player', Grandpa had always said.

The motor turned over with a roar and then settled down to a soft murmur. He was hunched forward over the steering-wheel, listening. 'One of the tappets needs adjusting,' he commented. 'Hear that little pockety-pockety sound?'

'Yes.' But I thought it was my heart, she told herself. What in the world is the matter with me?

'Not to worry, love. It won't rain on our parade. Here we go.'

And indeed there they went. Out on to Main Street, then further along to Route 28. The wind blew wildly. All the pins fell out of her hair, and ruined all the effort she had but moments ago put into combing it. But it felt—free? She almost shouted for joy as they cruised along the narrow back-roads and across rolling countryside until they came to the river, and the King of Prussia bridge. It was almost an afterthought when he pulled into a small lay-by above the river and parked. He leaned over towards her.

'Something's wrong?' she asked.

'Yes. Your seatbelt's too tight.' He leaned closer and unfastened both clips.

'I hadn't noticed. I don't need it for safety purposes?'

'I'm not all that sure,' he said as he pulled her across the wide seat until she was hard up against him. 'But there's only one way to find out.'

Kissing is a disease with this man, Leonie thought. But I'm too tired to object. That's a satisfactory lie, isn't it?

It must have been, because the moment his moist lips touched hers she relaxed entirely. All the load of tensions that had been on her shoulders for such a long time slid off. And fell into the river? she asked herself, laughing. It was almost an hour later when he moved an inch or two away from her. 'Maybe I was wrong,' he

said. 'Maybe we *do* need the seatbelts for safety purposes. For *your* safety.'

She almost felt like telling him not to be so safety-
cautious the next time around. Almost, but not quite.

CHAPTER SIX

LEONIE MARSHAL sat at the breakfast-table, slightly bent over as if all her troubles were too much for her. She held a paper in one hand, and a pencil in the other.

'Well,' Charlie Wheeler said. 'I didn't expect to find you up this early.'

Leonie looked up at him and mustered as much of a smile as she could manage. 'When you've been accustomed to being up and about at five o'clock,' she said, 'six-thirty seems to be the middle of the day. Good morning to you.'

'And good morning to you. What's up?'

Leonie held up her paper. 'A list of jobs advertised in the morning paper. Six possibilities, and none of them what I would call attractive. The only qualification I have for any of these six is that they call for a female.'

'And that you are,' he said enthusiastically as he pulled out a chair and sat down beside her.

Leonie blushed as she looked at him. It all sounded so—sincere. At least she meant to judge it that way. 'Coffee?' she offered. At his nod she got up from the table and went over to the percolator. Six-thirty in the morning and it was so dark that the red light on the coffee-pot gleamed loud and clear across the dimly lit room. She poured him a mug and returned to the table.

'Nice,' he said.

'The coffee? I've been making the family coffee since I was ten years old.'

'That long?' She nodded. 'But I hadn't really meant the coffee,' he said lazily.

'I don't understand you,' she said, sighing. 'At this hour of the day and you're still passing out compliments?'

'It never hurts.' His hand, warm from the coffee-mug, gently touched the back of her hand. She restrained the attempt to snatch it away. Even for a before-breakfast contact there was a certain pleasantness about that touch. But it *was* early. So she said so.

'Too early for romance?' he asked. 'Why, this is just the shank of the day. After w—after you get married, you're going to find there's nothing better than waking up early to find your husband beside you.'

'Morning mouth?'

'An overrated advertising pitch. There are ever so many things a man and a woman can do early in the morning to make one forget that toothbrush commercial.'

And just what would that be? Leonie asked herself. And kept the question strictly to herself. After running a farm all these years she knew exactly what he meant. But then again, she reminded herself, all my knowledge is theoretical. I've never really tried it out!

'Are you really all that desperate for a job?' he asked.

'Desperate? Yes, I guess that's the word. We're barely holding our heads above water at the moment. By Christmas, at this rate, we'll sink.'

'The auction didn't do as well as you expected?'

'We received a lot less than I expected, but Aunt Agnes has been studying prices for auctions throughout all the frontier counties, and she says we've done just about the average of all the others. It's a bad time for small farmers, that's all. The only people who might buy cows are either slaughter houses or other dairies. And at the moment there are only some three hundred dairies left operating in Massachusetts. I don't know where all the money's gone. I have a suspicion that it has something to do with this 'free trade' the President keeps talking about. And all I really know is that both of our shoe factories have moved to Taiwan.'

'You might be right,' he commented. 'But it's not hitting the service industries. That's why Wheeler's may be the rescue of this town.'

'Eventually,' Leonie admitted. 'But before we all starve to death?'

'Oh, I think it will be before then. But, come to think of it, I have a job you might consider. Part-time, of course.'

'Something I qualify for just because I'm a woman.'

'Exactly right,' he said, chuckling. 'You know that we've been working hard to upgrade our local store?'

'I can't say that I've noticed.'

'Well, I'll pay you to notice, Leonie. I need to have someone—some woman—take a tour of the local store from time to time, and give us a written report. How pleasant are the employees? How good is the fruit? Or the meat? How good is the lighting? How acceptable are the prices? Things like that. Interested?'

'Sort of an industrial spy?'

'More like a comparison shopper. All perfectly legal.'

'And if the store manager catches me?'

He shook his head slowly. 'Would you believe,' he said, 'I don't believe our local manager could catch cold in the middle of a flu epidemic? Interested?' And he told her how much he was willing to pay.

Leonie had just sipped at her own coffee. When he told her the amount she almost choked, and had to feel around for her napkin to keep from spitting up on the table cloth. He reached over and patted her on the back. If you could call that patting.

The air rushed out of her lungs in an explosion of sound. Her head rocked mightily. 'All right, all right,' she gasped. 'Don't murder me; I'll take the job!'

'That's fine. We have a checklist down at the office that we've been working on for a week. C'mon. I'll drive you in, and you can pick one up.'

'I—you want me to start immediately?'

'Like at once.'

'Yes, but——'

'But? Let's get started with enthusiasm, girl.'

'Yes, but it's only six forty-five—Charlie. Your office people can't possibly be in at this hour, and the store doesn't open until nine.'

And that's the first time I've ever called him by his first name, Leonie thought, and he hasn't even noticed! Or had he? His eyes had widened, and a curious look flashed across his broad face. 'And that's something else we'll have to do something about,' he murmured as he gazed down at her perky face.

'Like what?' she asked.

Like nothing can be done for two hours or more, he told himself. Like I could spend a very large part of that time kissing that very kissable face! And if I mention a word about it she'll be off and running as far as the New York border before I can get close enough to smooch. So he made up something else. 'Like maybe we need to consider keeping the store open twenty-four hours a day?'

He wasn't prepared for what happened next. Leonie settled back in her chair and laughed as if she had just heard the funniest joke in the world. 'It's not all *that* funny,' he complained.

'You've been a long time gone from the country,' she said as she tried to smother the giggles with a napkin. 'Farm people get up early to do the work, Charlie. But they go to bed early, too. I suppose you might find some in town who wanted to shop—oh, as late as nine o'clock at night, perhaps. But all night? Never happen!'

It was an argument a man could never win. But those giggles annoyed him, so he did the only thing possible to turn them off. He leaned over, caught her chin in one of his massive hands, and before she could escape he kissed her. Strange, he told himself some minutes later. She didn't even *try* to escape. And when he withdrew she almost looked forlorn! As if she was sorry it had all ended. It was an occurrence that gave Charlie Wheeler something to think about during the rest of his busy day.

Leonie spent the next hour trying to drum up all the experiences that might possibly fit into the advertised jobs. It was difficult. And having completed it she went up to her bedroom and considered her wardrobe. What did one wear while trying out for six different kinds of employment?

The answer was, Impossible. So she compromised by pulling out her navy blue trouser suit with the stippled lace blouse. And then spent almost half an hour trying to braid her unruly hair. Leaving the braid hanging made her look too young, so she compromised again, and pinned it all up into a glossy chignon. By eight o'clock she was ready to leave.

It was a strange sort of a day. The sun was struggling feebly with high fleeing clouds. The breeze was fitful and cold. Almost as cold as her first four stops in her job search.

Her fifth stop was at a honky-tonk down by the railroad station, and when the proprietor pulled out the uniform she would be expected to wear Leonie Marshal thanked him politely and went back on to the street. The proprietor followed her out to her car.

'Don't give up so easy, lady,' he said. 'Jobs are scarce. You could make a good weekly wage, believe me. You got nice boobs. Our clientele likes that sort of thing. But those glasses have gotta go.' He caught her wrist with one of his meaty hands.

There seemed to be only one thing to do. She shook her arm and managed to dislodge his hand. 'The glasses stay,' she said with a straight face. 'And my husband thinks the rest of me belongs to him too. He works over in the meat-packing plant in Seward.'

And, since meat-packing was about as tough a job as you could find in western Massachusetts, the man pulled back and left her to drive off in comparative serenity. She drove fitfully around the city. Her last possibility was a house-cleaning job, which she hated, and it was already eleven-thirty. She crumpled up the sheet of paper and headed straight for South Main Street and the DeMello building where once she had operated the playschool. She climbed up the old familiar stairs. They seemed both cleaner and wider than she remembered.

'Mr Wheeler?' the blonde receptionist said. 'I'm not sure that he's available. Do you have an appointment?'

'Yes,' she lied outright. 'Tell him I represent the Food for the Needy Committee.' The blonde did something with the complicated telephone on her desk. When she put down the handset there was a contemplative look on her face.

'Mr Wheeler doesn't remember the appointment,' she announced, 'but he's coming out to see you. He'll give you one minute, no more. Take a seat.' And with a 'so there' look on her face she swivelled around and turned her back on Leonie—who, not being the most mannerly girl in town, promptly stuck out her tongue at the imperial back. That was, of course, just the moment that

Charlie Wheeler popped through the door from the inner sanctum.

'Now just——' he started to say, and then he looked. 'Oh. Cat got your tongue?'

'Just practising,' Leonie said sweetly.

'And the Food for the Needy?'

Leonie stood up. 'That's me,' she said. 'It's lunchtime and I forgot my purse and I'm hungry as—I'm hungry. Doesn't that qualify me?'

He held out both hands in her direction, and tugged her into his arms. She could just barely see over his shoulder, to where the receptionist had whirled around to watch Leonie get her come-uppance. The girl's face sported an ugly look, suitable for framing.

I've got something she wants, Leonie told herself. And I wish I could keep him! But Charlie Wheeler was not the sort of man to let two women control the playing field. He took Leonie's upper arms, pushed her slightly away, and looked down at her quizzically.

'This isn't according to the script,' he said softly into her nearby ear. 'But yes, you get a free lunch, and it'll cost you.'

Leonie shivered. She had a suspicion that the price might be higher than she cared to pay. But she was hungry. Not just for food, but ready to throw her cap over the windmill. So she manufactured a carefree look, took his arm, and urged him in the direction of the stairs.

Something *had* been done to those stairs. They were able to walk down side by side, arm in arm. He opened the bottom door, the one she always required two hands and a prayer to operate, and he did it with one hand.

Suitably impressed, Leonie stepped out in front of him to the pavement, and was almost blown away by the increasing wind. 'Not to worry,' he called. 'Gotcha.'

And indeed he had, with one arm around her waist. So they walked up to Main Street, where the Frontier hotel maintained an old but gracious dining-room with large bay windows, from which they could watch newspapers and boxes and people all being blown in a southerly direction.

'Some day we have to get our town cleaned up,' Leonie said as the waiter pulled out a chair for her.

'Not a bad idea,' he commented as he sat down opposite her. 'What do you recommend?'

'A sort of town clean-up committee,' she replied.

'No. I mean what do you recommend to eat?' He handed her one of the ornate menus. She put it down beside her plate.

'You have three choices,' she told him. 'Chicken something or other, a chef's salad, or steak something or other.' He opened his menu suspiciously. 'The menu only changes four times a year,' she added.

'Chicken something or other?'

'It depends upon how George Syndron is feeling. He's the cook.' Leonie looked around like a conspirator. 'Look, take my advice. Order the steak. There's a slaughter house twelve miles from here——' She stabbed at her mouth with one hand, suppressing the added statement that 'her husband worked there'. That would certainly have wound his clock!

'And what about the steak?'

'It's fresh meat, properly aged, comes from a reputable slaughter house, and after all, what can a lousy cook do to a steak?'

He shrugged, and when the waiter came by ordered a medium-rare steak. And I've got to remember that, Leonie told herself. Who knows? Some day I might be cooking one for him myself!

'And *madame* will have?' The waiter bowed slightly, his pencil at the ready. All those little dreams faded.

'Oh, c'mon, Fred,' she said. 'I'll have the steak too.'

'Friend of yours?' Charlie Wheeler asked as the waiter walked away.

'Everybody is,' she said. 'It's a small place. Fred and I went to school together. He was the greatest tease in the high school.'

'But not any more?'

'Not any more.' Leonie grinned at him. 'Charlotte Wysinski took him in hand the year after they graduated. Fred is a suitably tamed husband these days.'

'Is that your goal, Leonie? To get a husband suitable for taming?'

'Who me?' she gasped. He reads minds, she told herself. Button up your lip, lady, before you put your foot in your mouth. 'Who me? I'm a liberated woman. I don't have my mind set on home and husband and children.' The fingers of both hands, resting on her lap, were crossed.

'But you might consider them?' He was leaning forward in his chair, and a fragment of a smile played around his lips.

Leonie fumbled, caught off guard. 'Well,' she finally said, 'if something extra special came along, I might consider it. That's the basis of our society, to hear the President say it. And you?'

'I'm not sure myself,' he said. 'I've tried it once before. To tell the truth, marriage isn't all it's chalked up to be.'

'You were married young?'

'Very young.'

'And what happened?'

'I'm not sure,' he said, sighing. 'Eventually she ran off with another man. But I can't say that it was all her fault. I was too busy working on my computer designs.

She suffered a lot of neglect. And so when the chance came she just vanished.'

'And she had no fault at all?'

'Oh, I wouldn't say that. I think that she could see the family fortune easier than she could see me. When she discovered we all had to work hard to keep it, things lost their flavour.'

'And Cecilia?'

'Ah, Cecilia. Cecilia was a mistake after a long drinking party. Carol never considered that there would be a baby to take care of. And the poor little tyke loved her mother like mad.' He shook his head and leaned back as the waiter came back with their meal.

'And little Cecilia loves you, too.' Leonie ducked her head and began with the steak. Out of the corner of her eye she could see that his head came up, and a surprised look raced across his face.

'You really think so?'

'She needs a lot of TLC from you. Tender Loving Care.'

He sighed and sat back in his chair. 'Something I know very little about,' he ruminated.

'You could learn,' Leonie said earnestly. 'You *need* to learn!'

He looked her in the eye for a moment that seemed like an hour, and then picked up his fork. The rest of their lunch passed quietly.

Back out on the street, where the wind was gusting even higher, Leonie pulled her jacket around her tightly. 'I've got the afternoon free, and the larder is almost empty,' she told him as she held on to his arm to keep from blowing away. 'If you want I could go over to the store and do that inspection that you spoke about.'

'You haven't any money,' he reminded her. Leonie shook her head.

'I meant that I don't have any money here,' she said patiently. 'My purse is locked up in my car. Besides, I do all my shopping with a credit card. Aunt Agnes insists. She claims that I'm the worst bookkeeper in town, but if I buy on a plastic she'll eventually get the correct figures. Let's walk.'

So they walked. Or almost flew. Once more the wind ate up Leonie's hairpins, and sent her long red hair streaming out behind her. He actually required two hands to open the downstairs door of the building. 'Come up for a minute,' he suggested. 'We have some copies of those checklists that I mentioned. And besides, you have to pay me for the lunch.'

'But I——' Leonie started to protest, but he was going up the stairs two at a time, and it took all the rest of her breath to catch up with him.

The blonde receptionist was still at her post. There was a tremendous smile for Charlie, who came into her little office first, and then a wrestler's-size scowl when she realised that Leonie was still among those present.

'There are several calls for you, Mr Wheeler,' the blonde said. She waved the several call slips at him as if he were a bull and she the matador. He waved her off. 'Later, Rachel, later. I have a critical commitment right now.'

He turned around and pulled Leonie over against him again. 'Oh, lord,' she murmured, 'am I to be blessed again?'

'Never mind the sarcasm,' he told her. 'There's the little matter about payment for the lunch.'

She managed, by dint of a great deal of luck, to push herself away far enough so that she could see his face. 'I told you,' she said firmly. 'My purse is still in my car. Must I go down and get it?'

'I don't think so,' he said lazily, and did away with that very little space between them. And he kissed her again. It started off as a gentle little salute, but in short order the tent caught fire. Leonie felt her control slipping, slipping, and then it was gone. Several hours later when he broke it off she was so weak from the brilliance of it all, she had to rest her head on his chest to get her breath back.

'Lord,' she whispered. 'If that's what the steak costs, I'm glad I didn't order any dessert.'

'You're a pretty lucky girl,' he returned. 'The shopping list is there on the table. Now get along and get the home fires burning.' He turned her around, pointed her towards the door, and gave her a little pat on her widest proportion as a starter. Leonie took a couple of stumbling steps, smiled sweetly at the receptionist, and with her feet at least six inches above the floor she made her way down the stairs and out into the wind.

Her car was half a block away. That half-block was a struggle, now that she was by herself. When she came up to the old station wagon she managed to get one of the doors open, using both hands, and slid into the driver's seat. It was another tussle to get the door closed again, but then the motor started, and the car was too heavy to be bothered by almost any size wind. Before driving off she took a good look at the checklist. It was very straightforward, and had the added advantage of requiring nothing but ticks. And so she drove over to the store.

'Everybody else in Fairview is watching the weather,' Leonie told herself as she came into the almost empty car park. 'Only dummies are out in this kind of wind.' She fingered her car radio, hoping to find a weather report, but her old car had a radio that was just too old for that. It squealed and hissed and then conked out completely.

She parked as close to the main doors as was possible, picked up her purse, pushed her glasses up on her nose, and struggled into the store. There were five assistants on duty, all of them crowded around the front windows, observing the build-up of the storm. Not another soul was shopping. And I'm going to go up and down all the aisles with my checklist? Leonie asked herself. Baloney.

So she scooted down the meat aisle, bought twenty-five dollars' worth of steak—which wasn't all that much meat, after all—and made her way back to the check-out counter where a nervous assistant punched out her charges. No sooner had that been finished and her meat bagged than the manager of the store came over.

'That's all, Rebecca,' he told the girl at the cash register. 'Tell the rest of them. The weather forecast is all bad. We're closing up immediately.' He gave Leonie a suspicious eye, and watched as she snatched up her plastic bag and card and ran for her car.

She came back from town just before two o'clock. There was a real chill in the air, with the weatherman forecasting the onslaught of a storm out of Canada. The Montreal Express, it was called in these western Massachusetts counties.

There was mail in the box set up on a steel pillar by the roadside. She stopped long enough to pick it up before she drove the old station wagon down into the driveway. The barn door was open, and she could see the yellow sheen of the antique Packard. There was another car parked beside it, a shiny black four-wheel-drive Cherokee. It seemed almost like an insult to drive her battered wagon in beside all this pristine beauty.

Tighe came to bark at her when she started back up the little hill. 'Been chasing rabbits?' she called as she bent to pet the ancient head. He wagged what might well have been agreement. He hunted relentlessly, but the only rabbit which could possibly run slower than he was a dead one, and, with the state his teeth were in, had he caught one he would have had to gum it to death. But he did try.

The dog followed her up the back stairs. Ordinarily he would have remained outside, but even the animal could recognise the coming of the storm.

The kitchen was crowded. Aunt Agnes and Cecilia were at the kitchen table playing cards. Charles Wheeler was sunk deep in her grandfather's old rocking-chair, reading the afternoon paper. They all looked up as she banged inside. The radio was playing from the shelf over the stove.

'I'm glad you're home,' her aunt said. 'They say——'

'There's gonna be snow,' Cecilia interrupted. 'Is that possible? Only the first week in November and already they say snow?'

'Anything's possible,' Leonie returned. She was struggling with her coat and her package of steaks; in a second big male hands were at her shoulders, helping her to shrug her way out of the tight old coat.

'It's too small for you,' he murmured in her ear as he swung the heavy coat off and away.

'Everything is,' she muttered disgustedly.

'Don't think I haven't noticed,' he returned. She looked over her shoulder quickly. He was looking down at her breasts, pushing to escape the confines of her old sweater. A shiver ran down her spine, having nothing to do with the storm outside. She shook herself free from his hands and moved over to the table.

'Any luck?' Aunt Agnes put down her cards for a moment and looked at her.

'Nothing,' she reported. 'Not a job to be had anywhere in the county, except for door-to-door sales-people, and I——'

'We're not that desperate yet.' Her aunt put her cards face down on the table and got up. There was a perked coffee-pot on the stove. Aunt Agnes went to it and poured a mugful for Leonie. 'Here. This ought to take the chill away.'

Leonie treasured the warm mug between her two hands as she moved closer to the table and peeped over Cecilia's shoulder.

'Oh, no, you don't,' the girl said as she ducked her cards out of sight. There was a broad grin on her gamin face.

'Mail,' Leonie announced as she dumped the lot on the table.

'You wouldn't know there's a recession running, not by the mail,' Charlie said as he came over and began sorting.

'Junk mail mostly,' Leonie returned. He was piling up all the advertising pamphlets in front of her.

'But this isn't,' Charlie said as he held up a small dirty envelope that Leonie almost remembered. 'You correspond with a convict?'

'What?' all three women in the room asked at the same time.

'This letter is from the state penitentiary.'

'Oh, cool,' Cecilia said.

'No, it's not "cool",' Aunt Agnes corrected her. 'Is it from the scoundrel?'

'You know a scoundrel? That's neat,' Cecilia was impressed.

'Come on, honey,' Charlie said as he led his daughter out of the room. 'I think I need to explain to you about scoundrels and their desirability.'

'What does this one say?' Aunt Agnes said quietly.

Leonie opened the envelope and read. 'I'm getting out in two days. I've got unfinished business there. I really want to see you. I'll be there soon. Love and kisses, Jeff.'

'I'm frightened, Leonie,' Aunt Agnes said. 'I don't like him. I never liked him. He scares me. I think we should tell Charlie. Don't you?'

'I'll tell him,' Leonie promised. 'When I get the opportunity. Oh, look, here's something else that's not junk mail. It's addressed to you.'

'Oh, my,' Aunt Agnes murmured. In a moment the old lady was smiling, waving a cheque in the air in front of Leonie's nose.

'Somebody's paying us something?' Leonie went around the table to stand behind her aunt to see better. Her glasses were fogged by the change from the cold outdoors to the warmth of the kitchen. She snatched up a tissue and began scrubbing them dry.

'That article that you wrote for *New England Magazine*,' her aunt chortled. 'Signed, sealed and delivered. And a cheque for two hundred and fifty dollars!'

'Now ain't that somethin'?' Cecilia crowed as she came back into the room. 'Daddy explained "scoundrel" to me. The lecture is over. It's really radical that we've got a writer in our midst.'

'Indeed so.' Charlie's bass voice underlined the goodwill in his daughter's voice.

'What was it about—the article, I mean?'

'A short story about giving up farming,' Leonie responded bleakly.

'Write what you know. Isn't that the instruction they give all first-time writers? Write what you know, young people. Only if you're young enough for that kind of direction, you're too young to know anything worth writing about.' She managed to get her glasses dried off and back on her nose. 'But it's nice. We can use the money.'

'I suppose you can take up the writing profession now?' Charlie asked.

Leonie grinned as she shook her head. 'They also say, Don't give up your day job too soon.'

'Oh, dear,' Aunt Agnes had gone on to the rest of the mail, and had just opened a large official-looking envelope. 'Oh, dear me.'

Leonie felt the weight of her tone. Something wrong. Something drastically wrong!

The room went quiet. So quiet that the ticking of the clock in the hall could be plainly heard. 'What?' Leonie asked cautiously.

Her aunt waved the paper in front of them. 'The sewer,' she gasped, and put the paper down.

'It's been approved? They're assessing for the construction?'

Aunt Agnes waved towards the paper on the table, but seemed unable to talk. Leonie looked down at it as if it were a coiled rattlesnake. Charlie Wheeler leaned over them all and picked it up. 'Shall I read it?' he asked.

Leonie, feeling sick to her stomach, nodded. 'Everything's been going so well,' she said, sighing. 'I thought we might be able to hold our heads up until Christmas. And now this.' She stabbed at her eye to hold back the tears. 'How much?'

'Fifty dollars a running foot,' he read, 'On all property facing on Main Street. Plus an installation fee of four hundred and fifty dollars for each house connection.' He dropped the paper back on the table in front of Leonie. 'That doesn't sound bad,' he said. 'Certainly it would be a big improvement to your property.'

'Yes,' Leonie agreed, trying to fight off the tears. 'Yes, it'll be a big improvement to the property, but first we have to face the bill. If we don't pay up the county will seize the whole place.'

'It can't be that bad. How much of your property fronts on the street?'

'Not much,' she responded. 'Three hundred and fifty feet. At fifty dollars a running foot?' It was too much arithmetic for her tired mind. But not for Aunt Agnes.

'Seventeen thousand, five hundred dollars,' the old lady said. 'Seventeen thousand, nine hundred and fifty if we opt for the house connection.'

'It might just as well be ten million,' Leonie murmured forlornly. 'I—can't pay it, and the bank won't loan me another cent! I don't know what to do——'

'It's snowing outside,' Cecilia interrupted, not at all concerned with things like sewers. The child rushed to the window.

'I don't suppose you'd be willing to loan me the money to clear the house—at market interest?' Leonie said, so quietly that only Charlie could hear.

'I—no, I couldn't get that much money up. Even for you.'

Leonie knuckled one eye dry and stared up at him. No, she told herself, he's got all his money tied up in launching the new stores. Otherwise he'd be glad to loan me the money. Wouldn't he? Another little shiver went up her spine. Maybe he wouldn't. Maybe he just wants to wait until the county auctions the farm off, so he can pick it up cheaply? Why am I so suspicious of him? Maybe I'm only daydreaming about love?

'There's another way,' he said, taking her hand. 'Let's get away from this crowd, shall we?' His gentle tug led her out of the kitchen and into the furthest corner of the big parlour, where he put his hands on both her shoulders and turned her around to face him.

'What else?' she asked, her face almost buried in his shirt.

'Simple enough,' he said. 'You could marry me!'

CHAPTER SEVEN

'MARRY you?'

'It isn't all that impossible to think of, is it?'

'You want me to marry you just to save my house?'

'Well, it's not that simple. Look around you. You badly need a cash infusion just to keep this little family afloat.'

'I admit that. What else is new?' She managed to push herself away from him, and took a moment to brush her long hair off her face. This is the man, she told herself. The man who ran me out of my playschool, the only real income I had. And started the avalanche that forced me to sell off my little dairy. And left me with—what do the police say? 'No visible means of support'!

She backed off into a corner of the room, folding her arms across her breasts protectively. The wind howled at the two windows behind her. By all real accounts, she thought, I should hate him. And he wants to *marry* me? At least I know it can't be for my money—or any other tangible assets, which I don't have any more. Unless he wants the whole farm?

The thought struck her full in the face. He wants the whole farm, not just the farmhouse and the barn! But——

'Then of course I need someone to help me care for Cecilia. You and she seem to be getting along marvellously these days. As does Aunt Agnes. How about that? In one fell swoop you get a husband, a grandmother, and a daughter. You can't beat that for progress, can you?'

Yes, how about that? Leonie screamed at herself. All these goodies for him, and in return I get a new sewer line. How romantic can I get? Of course, I've felt a little warm for him in the past week or two, but do my ears hear all the terms of endearment pouring from his side of the bed?

Of the bed. The thought sneaked up on her out of the blue. Of the bed? A necessary part of marriage, and how do you feel about that, Leonie Marshal? She could tell how she felt from the heat rising to her cheeks; he ought to be able to *see* how she felt as her face turned blush-red.

'I—don't——' she stammered, hoping for heaven to intercede. Which it did. There was a momentary lull in the wail of the storm. Just enough for both of them to hear the ugly crash of metal against stone from out on the highway.

'Somebody's hit something,' he said. 'Kill the lights.'

' "Kill the lights",' she snorted. Orders. I wonder how long it took him to get to be a general? But she went over to the wall anyway and did as ordered. He rushed to the window and pulled back the curtain.

'Damn,' he muttered as she came over to join him. 'Too much snow. I can't see as far as the highway. What's up there to hit?'

'The stone wall at our gate,' she reminded him. 'Although it's been there for seventy years and nobody's hit it yet.'

'There's always a first time. Come on,' he commanded. 'We've got to get out there and investigate. But first you'd better call the police.'

'I've told you before, there aren't any police in town, and in this weather it would take years for the state police to come over.'

'So an ambulance?'

'We don't have any of those, either. And no hospital. We had one but it closed.'

'Don't tell me there's no doctor?'

'Oh, there's a doctor all right. Jonas. But he's seventy years old, and I doubt if he could come out on a——'

'All right,' he interrupted. 'I get the picture. Get your boots on.'

'Please,' Leonie prompted as she started for the kitchen. He stopped, startled.

'Yeah. Please.'

Feeling a little better for it, Leonie marched out into the kitchen, where Aunt Agnes and Cecilia were back at their card game. Both of them looked up.

'So you've solved the problem,' Aunt Agnes said, peering at them over her glasses. There was a glint of expectation in her eyes.

'Yes,' Charlie Wheeler said, 'but——'

'No,' Leonie said very firmly, 'we certainly haven't, but there's been an accident up at the highway, and we're——'

'And I'm coming too,' Cecilia said as she slid out of her chair and ran for the clothes rack.

'The hell you are,' her father roared at her. But, ten minutes later, all bundled to the ears, there were three of them who pushed hard against the back door, almost locked in by drifting snow, and started to make their way up the smothered drive towards the street.

'Hold hands,' Charlie Wheeler roared back at them. 'Walk in my footsteps, and keep your scarves up over your noses and mouths.'

We hear and obey, Leonie thought to herself. Is this how it would be if I married him? Me chief, you squaw? Walk behind me. Carry the loads. She groped around at the side of the house and found her old sledge standing there. She had to operate by touch. Her glasses were already stormed over.

'Lucky I thought to clean this up last week,' she shouted at him. He stopped just long enough for a quick look.

'Yeah. Lucky. Come on. At this rate it'll be lucky if we reach the road by springtime.'

Yeah, she told herself. Yeah indeed. A little more sarcasm, Mr Wheeler, and your troops are going to rebel. But in a singular attack of cowardice she kept her mouth shut.

A moment later her foot slipped as her mind wandered. She missed stepping into his footsteps, skidded off to one side, and almost buried herself in the snow bank. The sledge bumped up on top of her.

'Well, you didn't have to knock me down too,' Cecilia complained.

'No, you're right, and I won't do it again.' Leonie was still sitting in the snow when a massive hand snatched at her arm and popped her out like a cork coming out of a champagne bottle. And then, as she stood quivering before him, the other massive hand began to beat her about the shoulders and back.

'All right,' she yelled at him. 'All right! I can——'

'Just trying to get some of the snow off of you,' he replied. 'Let's go.'

The wind had abated somewhat. The snow, instead of coming in sideways, was now drifting down in soft swirls from directly overhead. Some visibility was restored. They could see almost six feet in front of them. Directly in front of them the nose of a big black Cadillac was firmly embedded in the northerly edge of the stone wall, as if the driver had tried to make the turn into the driveway and failed by inches. A little wisp of steam spiralled up out of its pierced radiator.

Charlie stopped beside the car and began wiping the accumulated snow off the side-window and the wind-screen. Cecilia came up behind him and leaned against the fender. Leonie, with her head down, bumped into the child and pushed her up against her father.

'Watch it,' he said grumpily.

'Clumsy,' his daughter said as she straightened herself.

'Yeah, clumsy,' Leonie growled. 'It's a problem. Wait till you get as old as me.' She took a minute to clear the snow off her glasses.

'There's a woman in the car,' Wheeler commented as he struggled with the jammed door. 'Only one.'

'Who is it?' Leonie asked.

'How should I know? Whatever crazy who feels like driving on a night like this.'

'Lucky your lamp-post was lit,' Cecilia said. 'If this is the place she was going she just barely missed.'

'Bring that sledge over beside the door,' Wheeler commanded.

'I don't know anybody who'd be coming to my house,' Leonie gasped as she towed the heavy sledge around in a circle and parked it by the door. 'Not on a night like this!'

Charlie Wheeler had managed to force the driver's door wide open. He leaned into the car and carefully checked the victim. 'Only seems to be a concussion,' he told Leonie. 'Luckily she had her seatbelt on.' And then he put his back to it, and slid the car driver out and on to the sledge. 'No bleeding, and only a small bump,' he added.

'Maybe she's lucky,' Leonie commented as she moved to the back of the sledge. 'You pull, I'll watch from the back, and Cecilia, run ahead and have Aunt Agnes get the couch in the living-room ready. And something warm to drink, please. And my spare glasses.'

He had been bent over, tying the woman to the sledge. Now he lifted his head, barely six inches from Leonie. 'I hate bossy women,' he said fiercely, and started down the path they had ploughed on the way up.

'He means you,' Cecilia said, chuckling. Not waiting for an answer, she went off in front of the sledge.

Twins, Leonie told herself as she started off in the sledge's wake. Father and daughter, but twins. They have the same reactions, the same attitudes, the same bad tempers! I go to Mass every Sunday; how could God afflict me with a pair like this? God was apparently busy elsewhere, and didn't answer directly.

The trip back was a cinch. The wind had fallen off even further, the snowfall was heavy, but the flakes were tiny and light. Aunt Agnes was already at the door when the sledge bumped to a stop. Cecilia gave the slippery steps a hasty wipe, and then held the door for her father. With her usual good luck, Leonie tripped over the trailing edge of the sledge. By the time she made it into the kitchen the others were all crowded into the living-room, stripping the accident victim of her heavy clothing before they stretched her out on the big couch.

Not wanting to crowd into the fray, Leonie shrugged herself out of her outdoor things and hung them all on the hooks beside the door, to dry out. Her hands were half frozen. She walked over to the radiator and stole some of the warmth. Her glasses were useless; she took them off and fumbled them on to the kitchen table. It was suddenly very quiet in the living-room.

Driven by curiosity, Leonie wandered over to the big double door that separated living-room from kitchen. 'Something wrong?' she asked. 'Should I call the doctor? Do you know who it is?'

'She's unconscious,' Charlie Wheeler reported. 'Yes, call the doctor. We can probably use some advice over the telephone.'

'It's my mother,' Cecilia announced. There was a tremor that might be fear in the girl's voice.

'It seems like midnight but it's only eight o'clock,' Aunt Agnes said as she came out to the kitchen. 'Decaf coffee? I wouldn't want anything to keep me awake tonight. I don't feel up to climbing the stairs again, either. How is she?'

'As well as can be expected,' Leonie replied. 'That's a fancy medical term I picked up when I talked to Dr Jonas. Her temperature is normal, she's in the middle of a normal sleep cycle, and I can't find anything else wrong with her except for that bump on her forehead.'

'Hit her head on the steering-wheel? Did she have her seatbelt on?'

'Apparently. Lucky. Now if it were me I would have rammed my head through the windscreen, seatbelt or not.'

'Don't run yourself down, child,' the old lady said as she sank into a chair at the table. 'You're not so overrun with bad luck as all that. What else did the doctor say?'

'He said there's always the possibility of a concussion. We're to keep her in bed for two or three days, just in case. If the roads are ploughed, he'll come by himself for a look-see.'

'And—it's true what Cecilia said?'

'Yes.' Leonie brushed her hair back in an unconscious gesture of concern. 'His ex-wife.' And if that isn't my usual bad luck, she told herself. At three o'clock he proposes to me. By seven o'clock he's all wrapped up with his wife. His *ex*-wife, I suppose I should say. And Charlie

Wheeler's drooling over her as if she were the latest Miss America!

'Mr Wheeler's been sitting up there at her bedside since five o'clock. We put her in the bedroom next to his. And Cecilia's on the other side. A nice family gathering.'

'I suppose we're lucky to have them all,' Aunt Agnes murmured. Leonie winced. Her aunt, who knew more than a few things about people and psychology, noted the expression, and concluded that the game being played within these walls was not necessarily over. Neither for Leonie, nor—— 'I forget. What did you say her name is?'

'Carol.' Said glumly, as if it were a name reserved solely for lepers.

Neither for Leonie nor Carol, Aunt Agnes continued her thought.

'I know the clock says it's early, child, but I'm tired. I think I'll make one more trip upstairs, and then to bed. Don't you sit up late.' She got up slowly, rinsed her coffee-mug and set it on the sideboard, and then headed for the stairs.

Look at that, Leonie told herself. Aunt Agnes is growing older by the minute! The best aunt I've ever adopted! I mustn't let all my problems slop over on her. There were footsteps on the stairs. Old ones, going up slowly; young ones, coming down two stairs at a time. Cecilia.

The young girl slipped into one of the kitchen chairs.

'Want some supper?' Leonie asked.

'Maybe—you don't suppose I could have a sandwich to eat in the living-room? There's a TV show I want to watch in about half an hour.'

'No problem. A ham sandwich? You look tired, friend.'

'I—I don't know what to make of things,' Cecilia confessed. 'I haven't seen my mother for a long time, and now——'

'Here she's dropped down the chimney, huh?' Leonie was still having trouble with her glasses. The storm immersion had done them no good. One of the eye-pieces was now slightly askew.

'I thought—Aunt Agnes and me, we thought—well, we had no business thinking like that. But there's one thing I'm sure of about my mother: she never would have come if she didn't want something. What do you suppose she wants?'

'Your father?' Leonie asked quizzically.

'I don't think so. They had the most god-awful arguments. It would be nice if they were back together, wouldn't it? But I don't see that happening. I know lots of kids with divorced parents. None of them ever got remarried to each other.'

'Is that what you hope for?'

'I ain't that much of a nut. It would be nice, though, if Dad did get married. I don't mean to my mother, you understand. Any nice girl would do.'

'You're a very broad-minded person,' Leonie commented. 'And very nice. Scoot into the living-room and I'll bring you your sandwich.'

'Don't get me wrong,' the child said as she pushed back her chair. 'Nice I ain't. Nice people always come in last. My dad said that once.'

'And your dad is never wrong?'

The child hmmphed and left Leonie behind, shaking her head. How come, Leonie asked herself, the modern kid is so much smarter than I was at that age? She pushed back her own chair and headed for the refrigerator. The ham, naturally, was at the back of the fridge, behind four pints of milk, a plastic pickle container, and half a dozen tiny containers of left-overs.

'Never throw anything away?' He was standing directly behind her left ear.

Leonie jumped. Four of the little containers fell from her hands and made plopping noises on the floor as their covers fell off. The sound attracted Tighe, who began a massive clean-up with his tongue. 'Don't *do* that,' she gasped. 'You'll scare the daylights out of me!'

'That'll be a cold day in spring,' Charlie Wheeler commented. He leaned over the top of the refrigerator door and looked in. 'Ham?'

'Ham.'

'That'll be fine. How's the storm making out?'

'Slowing. The radio said it would be over by dawn. None of the major streets and highways has been ploughed yet. The town manager says it would be a waste of time to send the ploughs out now.'

'Ploughs, plural?'

'Of course. Snow is a constant part of our winter life up here. Our town has two of our own, and the state ploughs the major highways. But not right away. I have this political theory.'

He waited for a moment, grinning at her as she shifted the load in the refrigerator and finally managed to get the ham and the mayonnaise out.

'And your theory is?' He relieved her of her load and put them on the kitchen table.

'My theory is,' she said triumphantly as she came up with the pickles, 'the speed of political reaction is directly related to the distance between the location and the State House at Boston.'

'Possibly,' he acknowledged. 'Where's the bread?'

'That's what I like about big tycoons,' she told him. 'The bread is in the bread-box. And if you would kindly move aside I'll get these sandwiches constructed.'

She worked diligently for a few minutes, taking an occasional peek at him from under her wildly swirling hair. 'And you know something else I've heard?' she teased. He grinned at her. 'Boys who are fully able to feed themselves at fourteen find that the skill completely atrophies at twenty-five if there's some female around to do it for them. Would you believe that?'

'Sarcasm will get you nowhere,' he grumbled. 'Hold still. You've got some mayonnaise on your nose.'

'I'll be darned if I have. Do I?' She put down her knife and straightened up.

'Of course you do. Hold still.' He came around the table and tilted her chin up with one of his fingers. 'There,' he said. 'Right on the tip of your nose.'

'I'll——'

'I'll get it,' he interrupted, and before she could duck he kissed her—and then very gently licked the wandering bit of sandwich dressing from the tip of her upturned nose.

'Don't,' she sputtered as she tried to back away. His breath had fogged her glasses again.

'Don't? After all we've been to each other this week?'

'No. Don't,' she squeaked.

'We've done it before, why not now?'

'But we've never had your wife upstairs before.'

'Damn you,' he snapped. '*Ex*-wife!' And he proceeded to kiss her again. But this time it was neither short nor gentle, and passion snatched at Leonie Marshal's heart.

Dawn came on leaden skies. The clouds were only slightly lighter than they had been on the previous day, but the snow had ceased. Leonie crept downstairs, only to find a gathering at the kitchen table. They all looked up at her with eyes that were sleep-laden.

'You couldn't sleep either,' Aunt Agnes stated. She offered a brief salute with her coffee-mug.

'I got a headache,' Cecilia commented. A cup of hot chocolate steamed in front of her, but she was paying no attention to it.

'Me too, but more than just one,' Charlie Wheeler said. He leaned both elbows on the table and studied Leonie as if she were some new species of animal just come up out of the swamp. She came to a stop at the door of the kitchen and looked him over.

What you see is what you get, she reminded herself. His hair was all awry, and the dull blue of his unshaven face looked as if it was barbed wire. Leonie had seen many a farm hand in similar circumstances, but this was *her* man. She walked around the table, and, just to be sure, ran a finger down the side of his cheek.

'You're right,' he said, almost as if he were reading her mind. 'Sandpaper. Don't get too close.'

She snatched her hand back, having forgotten that trick of his of anticipating what she thought.

'Sit down here,' Aunt Agnes offered. 'I'll get you a cup of coffee.'

'She couldn't get it herself?' Cecilia asked. 'Why doesn't she say something?'

'Because Leonie Marshal requires two cups of coffee every morning before she's fit to talk to anybody.' Aunt Agnes got up and went over to the stove. 'A fresh pot, love.' She poured a mugful and carried it over to where Leonie was sitting, hunched up in her chair with her battered green robe bound tightly around her.

'Definitely, what you see is what you get,' Wheeler interjected.

Leonie's head snapped up and she glared at him, unwilling to speak. You're no prize yourself, she wanted to tell him. But truth intervened. And neither am I. We'd make a good pair, wouldn't we? Except that you have that—encumbrance—upstairs. I'll bet that when she comes down she'll look a fright as well.

The trouble with prophesying was that it was often wrong. As now. There was a clatter from above. Everyone at the table whirled around to look as Carol Wheeler came around the curve in the stairs and stopped to pose.

Oh, Gawd, Leonie cried at herself. Why me?

'Good morning.' A sweet, low voice, enough to charm angels. Leonie's heart fell a little further. And then a bit of dramatic art. The woman on the stair took another step down, her hand firmly on the banister, and then she lost her balance. At the very first waver Charlie Wheeler was up out of his chair, dashing for the swaying figure—and dumping what remained in his coffee-mug in Leonie's lap.

The coffee was still relatively warm, so it distracted Leonie for a moment or two. When she had recovered her aplomb she looked up into the stairwell. Charlie Wheeler, the primitive male triumphant, stood on the fifth stair with Carol in his arms, grinning like the monkey who had snatched the golden prize.

But Cecilia, facing the same scene, had risen from the table and backed across the room until she was hard up against the kitchen window. And the look in her eyes was something less than pleasant. Leonie's mind flew back to that moment of confession some days before. 'My mom didn't want me either'. Poor, poor child, she thought. No wonder Cecilia has more than enough aggression in that chunky body of hers to fight off the world.

'There now, I've got you safe.' Charlie Wheeler came down the stairs, his former wife cradled in his arms.

'I know you have,' Carol said as she scanned the rest of the group. 'I've always been safe with you.' The words dripped honey.

'I wonder what she wants?' Aunt Agnes whispered. Leonie shrugged her shoulders. But old-fashioned New England etiquette required that something be done.

'Set her down here,' Leonie said as she pulled out a chair next to the one Charlie had vacated so quickly. 'Do you feel well enough for breakfast? I'm sorry, we haven't been introduced. I don't know your name.'

Wheeler tucked her into the captain's chair with a great deal of solicitude. 'Carol,' the woman said as she offered a limp hand in Leonie's direction. 'Carol Wheeler.'

There was hardly room for Leonie to exchange a word. The woman turned to Charlie, who had resumed his seat between Leonie and Carol. 'Am I ever so glad to find you, Charles. I was afraid that I wouldn't, you know.' And then, over her shoulder to Leonie, 'I'd like coffee with milk, no sugar, and a piece of toast—lightly done.'

'I wouldn't have known where to look, Charles, except that your nice lawyer friend gave me your address. I was surprised. A man of your talent living in a boarding house. Quaint, of course, but still a boarding house.'

'We've made a great many improvements,' Leonie said sarcastically. 'We even have hot water. And by next month we'll be connected to the county sewer.'

Carol Wheeler drew herself up an inch or two and looked down her patrician nose. 'Sewer?'

Charlie frowned. Aunt Agnes kicked Leonie's foot under the table as she got up and went for coffee. Leonie studied Carol, wondering where it would be best to stick the knife. Five feet three or four, one hundred and ten pounds, blonde curly hair, and a sharp face, with nose and chin as the cutting edge. A lovely woman, who immediately turned the other way, showing her back to Leonie. A lovely back, Leonie thought. *That's* where I'll stick the knife.

'I can't imagine what brought you out in this storm,' Charlie was saying as Aunt Agnes planted a coffee-mug in front of Carol. The woman stirred the coffee gently, then laid the spoon down.

'I'm more accustomed to cups rather than mugs,' she commented. 'I've developed a serious business problem, Charles. Can we talk?'

'Go right ahead.'

'Privately, I mean. How long will we have to stay here?'

'The doctor said you shouldn't be up and around for a couple of days, Carol. Just in case you might have had some slight concussion.'

'Ah. Then I wouldn't want to take a chance. But I'm not sure—you remember how delicate my stomach is. The cooking——?'

'Is the best in the whole state,' Cecilia said.

'It surely is,' Charlie contributed. 'Best I've had in years.'

A tiny shudder ran across Carol's classical face. It'll sink a thousand ships, Leonie thought as she watched. And I noticed that Charles. Not Charlie. My, how sweet we are! Why am I so damn jealous?

Carol Wheeler sipped at the coffee and took a tiny nibble from the toast. 'And where are all my clothes, Charles?'

'Still in the car, I suppose,' he responded. 'We'll have to get your things out——'

'We'll have to get your car out too,' Leonie commented. 'It's blocking the driveway completely. Even if they plough the roads there's no way we could get into town for fresh groceries.'

'Don't anticipate troubles,' Aunt Agnes ordered. 'First we need to get Mrs Wheeler back to bed, then get her clothes, and after that we can see about her car.'

'I—hate to go back up those stairs,' Carol complained. 'Isn't there some place down here where I could rest?'

'Why, of course,' Aunt Agnes said. 'We have a very large sofa-couch in the parlour, and the heat's particularly good in there. Would you like that?'

'And a television set?'

'They got just the one,' Cecilia interjected. 'It's in the parlour.'

'Ah. Cecilia, darling. Come give mother a kiss.'

The girl responded strangely. She sidled around the table, and approached her mother as if she thought the woman might bite. When one of those smoothly powdered cheeks was offered, the child pecked at it and then quickly backed off. There was no hug asked or offered.

'Where was I?' the blonde asked. 'Oh, yes, the couch. Is there some privacy there?'

'The door closes,' Aunt Agnes said. 'There are curtains on the windows, and nobody lives within five hundred yards of the place.'

And isn't that a little bit of sarcasm, Leonie thought. Little Mrs Wheeler is beginning to get under my aunt's skin. And that takes some doing. When classes in Agnes Stone's last years of teaching, had risen to thirty-five students, Ms Stone had been noted for her equanimity.

'You'll enjoy it here,' Charlie said. 'The couch opens up into a queen-size bed.'

'But it's the only television set in the house,' Cecilia repeated. Her mother frowned at her. So did her father.

'Let me get clean sheets and open up the couch,' Aunt Agnes said. 'Cecilia can come and help me.'

The girl was obviously not that much in favour of helping, but she went grudgingly when the older woman seized her hand and tugged. Carol watched her daughter being towed out of the room.

'I had forgotten how—chunky she is,' she commented. 'I had hoped she might be more—swan-like. It was almost impossible to introduce her into society.'

'She's only nine years old,' Leonie protested. Both of them gave her glacial looks. I could run out in the snow and warm up, Leonie thought. Better still, I could keep my mouth shut. How about that?

She struggled up from the table. The lap of her robe was still wet, but she dared not shed it. Her nightgown was just a little—frivolous. The pair of them were talking in low voices, too low to be heard. Leonie bustled over to the sink, collected the dirty dishes and silverware, and dumped them all into hot water. It took but minutes to complete the washing and drying. She hung the little towel up on the rack over the sideboard and looked around. Everything was as neat as a pin, except for the spilled coffee on the floor by her chair.

Trying to look invisible, Leonie collected mop and cleaning materials, and ducked down below the table to work. A moment later Charlie Wheeler lifted the corner of the tablecloth and ducked his head down beside her.

'What the hell are you doing now?'

'I'm cleaning the floor where the coffee spilled.'

'What coffee spilled?'

'The stuff you spilled all over me when you ran off to do your Tarzan imitation.'

'I spilled coffee on you?'

'Hot coffee. It's cooled off now.'

'Oh, lord,' he muttered. 'When am I going to stop abusing you?' Leonie gave him a quizzical look, and then decided flight would be better than fight.

'Excuse me,' she said, and wiggled her way out from under the table and headed for the stairs. 'And now, if nobody minds, I'm going to get dressed.'

'Nobody minds,' he said. He sounded disgusted. With himself? Leonie swung herself up on to the second step, using the banister as a base.

'What a queer little thing she is,' Carol commented.

'But I have exceptional hearing,' Leonie said under her breath as she dashed up the stairs.

'Not all that little,' Charlie said as Leonie disappeared around the bend of the stairs. 'Not so little at all, for a fact.'

But by that time Leonie had disappeared from sight, and was even out of range for those superior ears of hers. If she *had* heard she might have felt more than a little bit better about the whole affair.

CHAPTER EIGHT

LEONIE managed to contain herself until the door of her room closed behind her, and then her temper burst through. Her favourite huge teddy bear sat on the floor by the foot of her bed. She came at it like a soccer striker preparing for the world cup. The bear flew across the room and flattened itself against the window. One of her three pillows followed. There were no tears—just a face flushed red and a wild desire to kill the man. Who is downstairs in *my* parlour, billing and cooing with his former wife, she told herself grimly.

Her robe was still coffee-wet, but she ignored it and dropped on the foot of the bed, chewing her bottom lip. So I can't kill him, she reasoned. He owns the only grocery store in town and the whole town would starve to death, right? She popped up off the bed and picked up her hairbrush. One hundred strokes, on a head of hair that was thick enough to be a tawny jungle. She applied her muscles, trying to wear herself out, wishing it were *his* head and her brush were a chain-saw!

About halfway through the ritual something scratched at her door. Tighe, she thought, come to commiserate with me—or come, a coward like me, to run away from the confusion?

She opened the door to find herself only half right. Tighe indeed, and Cecilia too. 'Can we come in?' The girl looked dishevelled and tired, as if she had been mentally battered.

'Of course.'

132

Her dog made straight for the rug that Leonie had braided when she was ten years old. Under her grandmother's supervision, of course. The little girl stomped across the room to peer out of the window, and then collapsed, sprawled out on the bed.

'That man!' The girl spat it out as if the words all had a bad taste.

'Yes,' Leonie agreed. She would have agreed with anything derogatory about Charlie Wheeler at this point. She put her brush back to work.

'You got beautiful hair.'

'Thank you. You have too, but you have to brush it every day. One hundred strokes, my mother used to say, but I was too little in those days to count up that high.'

'I can count to two hundred.'

'Good for you.' Leonie winced as she ran into a snarl that refused to untangle.

'Are those two gonna sit in the parlour all day?'

Leonie stopped long enough to take a good look at the child. She was dressed, as always, in blouse and jeans and shoes. No socks, even on this intemperate day. A tough little square block of a person, almost four feet high, weighing perhaps eighty pounds.

'You don't care to have them sit together?'

'No, I don't. I've learned a lot about parents in the last year or so. These two don't deserve each other. And besides, two of my favourite afternoon television shows are on this afternoon.'

'That's a *great* argument,' Leonie commented as she went back to the brush. 'Your mother and father can't talk in the parlour because you're missing your television?'

The girl sighed and sat up. The bed springs creaked loudly enough to jar Tighe loose from his rug. He grumbled a protest, walked to the head of the bed, and curled himself up on the bare floor. 'It sounds sorta selfish, doesn't it?' she said. 'But it's true. My mother is a schemer, and my dad's a nice man who's not smart enough to see what's good for him.'

'Luckily he's got you,' Leonie said sarcastically. 'That's a pretty biased idea you've got there.'

'Biased? I don't know what that means, but there's a word for the pair of them, only I don't quite remember. Incomp—something like that?'

'Incompatible?' Leonie suggested. I believe it, why shouldn't the kid? she asked herself. And the immediate answer popped up. Because the kid is Carol's daughter, and nobody ever forgets their mother. Do they?

'Yeah. Incompatible. I overheard my dad a couple of years ago, talking to Grandfather on the telephone. My mother and father had just had a terrible whopper of a shouting match, and my mother stormed out of the house. Then Dad said to Grandpa, "We're going to have a great marriage. Just as long as I can provide the income, she guarantees that she'll remain pattible."' The child paused, cocked her head, and looked up at Leonie. 'Funny?'

'Not exactly, Cecilia. Not exactly. That's what we call black humour.'

At which, to Leonie's surprise, the little girl doubled over and cried up a storm. The tension was too much for Tighe. The old dog got up and made for the door, asking to be let out. Leonie obliged, and then went over to the bed and sat down beside the child. For a moment Cecilia stiffened, and then her body collapsed against Leonie's as the tears continued to fall.

Leonie hesitated, then put one arm around Cecilia's shoulders and made soothing noises. No words, just noises. And while doing it her mind squirrelled around looking for a better solution. What *do* you do when a child is all broken to pieces like this? she wondered. Her eyes wandered to the window, and she smiled.

'Snow,' she said.

'What?' The child lifted her head up off Leonie's shoulder and made a stab at shutting down the waterfall.

'Snow,' Leonie repeated. 'The storm is over. We've got about two feet of the stuff lying around. Somebody's got to go out and shovel a path from here to there. How about that? You and I? Or is it you and me?'

A smile worked its way through the tears, like a rainbow after a storm. 'Us,' the child said. 'Let's go.'

'After I get dressed,' Leonie said. 'And after you change into something much warmer than that. Meet me in one hour, downstairs in the kitchen.'

'One hour,' Cecilia asked suspiciously. 'What do I do in one hour besides put on some socks?'

'What you do,' Leonie told her as she checked the back of the child's ears, 'is take the bath that you didn't get yesterday—or the day before, now that I think of it. And this time try a little soap.'

'There's nothing I hate worse than *rememberers*,' Cecilia announced as she flounced towards the door. But she was smiling, Leonie told herself, as she turned around to get herself in order.

Aunt Agnes was back at the kitchen table struggling with her second cup of coffee when Leonie came down. On any normal day she required a three-mug transfusion before she could start the day off.

'Oh, my,' she commented.

'Oh, my? What's that in order of?'

The old lady gestured vaguely at the green and gold combination Leonie was wearing. 'You're dressed for an afternoon at your social club. And don't ever end a sentence with a preposition. And you had better button a

couple more buttons on that blouse. It looks a little—
low. What's going on?'

'Oh, this thing? Just an old thing that I happened to
have in my closet. I thought I would——'

'He's still in there with his wife,' Aunt Agnes
interrupted.

Leonie flushed. 'How I dress has nothing to do with
him,' she said very severely. 'And she's *not* his wife.
Cecilia and I are going out to shovel snow.'

'From here to there? We don't need any paths. Nobody's going anywhere.' Aunt Agnes downed the last of
her coffee and got up to fetch a refill. With a fresh cup
in hand she looked Leonie over. 'La-di-da,' the older
woman said, chuckling. 'Dressing for the snowman, hey?
Not a bad idea. At least you won't get any smart answer
back from snowmen. What are you planning to do about
her car?'

'Well, I don't know, do I?' Leonie grumbled. 'A
Cadillac makes a very effective barrier. But at least we
can bring her suitcases in. She looks rather overdressed
wearing my other robe. It's almost half a foot too long
for her. What is she wearing for a nightgown?'

'I understand it's one of his shirts.'

'I'm ready,' Cecilia said as she exploded into the
kitchen. The girl took a look at the half-closed door of
the parlour. 'They're still at it?'

'I guess you might say that,' Aunt Agnes said. 'Going
shovelling, huh?'

'What could they be talking about all this time?' the
child asked. 'Before they got their divorce they hardly
ever spent any time talking. Are they smooching or
something?'

'I hardly think we could know,' Aunt Agnes returned.
'The door prevents anyone from seeing, my ears aren't

good enough for me to hear, and my mind rejects such blatant intrusion.'

So intrude, Aunt Agnes, Leonie said to herself. Intrude. This is one devil of a time for your New England morality to take over. I desperately need to know. At least listen from time to time! A slight bit of snooping is hardly a federal case.

She looked the entire speech at her elderly non-relative, but Aunt Agnes, who could read a face as easily as she could read a balance sheet, shrugged and urged them out. 'Have a good day, and be careful of frost-bite.'

'Yeah, careful,' Leonie grumbled as she led the way out on to the back porch and stopped to see that Cecilia was really bundled up.

'The shovels are under the porch,' Leonie announced. 'And that's our first problem. We don't have any shovels to dig out the shovels.'

But there was a way. It consisted of rolling snowballs from the little drift that isolated the porch storage area, and beginning a snowball war. As a result of which, by the time they managed to get two shovels they were both out of breath. They sagged down on the bottom step, just in time to hear the back door open and close above and behind them.

'Your dog doesn't care to come out,' Charlie Wheeler said. 'Is that all the shovelling you've managed so far?'

Cecilia bounced up to greet her father. Leonie would have liked to do the same, but hadn't the energy. Besides, she reminded herself, I'm full-out angry with the man. Double-dealing man.

'Did you have a pleasant conversation with your wife?' she asked.

Before he could get in a word his daughter interrupted. 'What did Mama want to say, Daddy? Are you two going to get back together again?'

There you go, kid, Leonie thought. Push him. Then I won't have to be so nosy, and still find out what I want to know. Nag him!

'I think that's premature thinking, Ceci,' he answered. 'Your mother has an interesting problem, and I'm not able to discuss it until we come to some settlement.'

'Not even a hint?'

'Not even a hint, baby.'

'I am *not*,' the child said firmly, 'a baby.'

'No, you're not, are you?' he said. 'Now, how about a little shovelling? Your mother needs her clothes, and they're all in the trunk of the Cadillac.'

The pair of them, father and daughter, moved up to the head of the drive, laughing where he had to lift her out of the snowbanks. The car was completely covered, with snow standing five or six inches high on its roof, and the boot completely out of sight.

'I'm going to start at this end,' Leonie called. Neither of them paid her the slightest attention, which did her ego no good at all. She shook her head, and decided to pitch in.

The house was located in a slight declivity, facing east. The storm had roared in from the north. As a result, the driveway on the south side was almost bare close to the house, but with wind-driven snowbanks almost reaching to four feet on its outer edge. The snow was light and dry, with only a patch or two where ice had formed. It was on these snowbanks that Leonie began her attack.

For almost a month now her muscles had been idle. No swinging the heavy milk cans, no handling the heavy feed bags. Her first few swings of the shovel let it be known that it would be no easy task. But after the initial warm-up she began to work up a rhythm. Occasionally she stopped to see how her competition was doing.

Cecilia was doing her best to clear the front of the car, pushing down the piles of snow on the roof, cleaning the windscreen, clearing an area around the two front wheels.

At the back of the car, where Charlie Wheeler was working, the man himself was almost invisible. His shovel was working so enthusiastically that a light cloud floated back on him from every load he threw off into the corner of the yard. At this rate, Leonie sighed, they'll be finished in twenty minutes, and I'll take twenty days!

'I'll get the outside of the car, as well,' Charlie called down to her.

'No,' Leonie yelled. 'Don't——'

She didn't have to explain why. At that very moment a pair of county snow-ploughs came down the highway at speed. They tootled their horns as they came up to the house, pleased to see someone else alive in the pristine whiteness of their world. And after they had gone by their parallel blades piled a snowbank up on the outside of the Cadillac which was so high that the car was completely buried again.

Leonie, who by that time had barely cleared three running feet of the drive, gave up her lonely venture and towed her shovel up to where the other two were working.

'Friends of yours?' Charlie asked as he waved to the now distant trucks.

Two things were plain to Leonie. He thought they must be her friends because they were trouble-makers, and he hated Leonie's friends. Thanks a lot, God, she muttered, and then quickly reversed herself. There is no need, she lectured herself grimly, to invoke the Deity in what is strictly a local problem. Besides which, you don't have all that many friends, Leonie Marshal.

'They're all county employees,' she said. 'But even if they were from Fairview it wouldn't have made any difference. That's the way ploughing is done up here in frontier country.'

He stopped to catch his breath. The temperature had dropped as a cold front chased after the storm, and he had wrapped a scarf around the lower part of his face. Clouds of white exhaust found their way through the scarf and out into the bright world. There was always a silver lining; with the cold front came clearing skies.

'Lovely area, Fairview,' he commented. She was no longer able to tell sarcasm from fact. 'I guess I might be better off starting up down-state. Or over by the ocean on the Cape.'

'It never snows here until after Thanksgiving,' she said, trying to explain away the unexplainable.

'That's supposed to cheer me up? What is this, whipped cream?'

'Well—I——' Leonie squeezed her eyes shut to stop the tears. That stupid stammer that had haunted her childhood was back with a vengeance. Get control of yourself and speak slowly, that was the cure. But it made her sound so solemn. 'But your daughter doesn't have to go to school. And I suppose you don't have to go in to your office?'

He bent down to shovel some more. 'The boss never gets time off,' he yelled at her.

It was the yelling at her, of course, that ruined things, and caused her glasses to fog up. And that, she told herself, is about the poorest run of logic ever *logicked*. She threw her shovel down without paying attention to where it might land.

'Ouch,' he yelled. 'Why, you little idiot. What are you trying to do, brain me?'

Leonie whipped off her glasses. Her handkerchief was in the pocket of her blouse. She could hardly get it to clear off the spectacles without undressing. And she was

so mad. 'It can't hurt what you haven't got,' she roared
back at him, and then turned away and stumbled down
the path.

Except that it wasn't the path. Without her glasses she
couldn't tell path from snowbank, and walked herself
right into the deepest depth of snow. Naturally she
slipped. Naturally her glasses fell out of her hands.
Naturally the world had no focus, and there was nothing
to touch that would restore her sense of place. 'God,
how I hate you,' she screamed.

And in that tiny moment he was with her, lifting her
up out of the snowbank, brushing her down gently,
holding her close so that her cold cheek was against his
warmth. 'Leonie,' he murmured in her half-frozen ear.
'Leonie, girl, why in the world do I do these things to
you, love?'

He was a big man, clothed for the outdoors. There
was just no way she could reach her arms around him.
No way in the world. But she tried. And then she hung
in his arms, her mind racing. 'Do these things to you'?
A guilty conscience running amok in the snow? 'Love'?
Probably just a buzz word used carelessly by people from
big cities like Springfield. Or Worcester. Or even Boston.

But from wherever it came, it didn't mean *love*, as in
'I love you'. Not a chance of that. She gave herself a
mental shake and tried to push away from him.

'Stand still,' he commanded, 'while I try to find your
glasses.' She felt the warm touch of lips on her forehead.
His big, looming, unfocused presence moved away from
her.

Give me some more orders, she snarled to herself. Go
ahead, big man! She tried to think of some way to hurt
him. Nothing physical. She wasn't capable of that, and
didn't want to anyway. Words were her weapons. 'You'd

better watch out. Your wife is watching through the parlour window.'

The big shape was back. 'What in the world are you talking about, woman?'

'I'm talking about—I don't know what I'm talking about. Did you find my glasses?'

'I'm cleaning them off.' The cold chill of plastic and metal settled on the tip of her nose. She pushed them higher up, and her world came into focus again. A big man. A big, angry man.

'Sometimes I wish you were a man,' he hissed. 'I'd give you such a knock!' His hands fell on her shoulders and gave her a shake or two, and then in a softer tone he said, 'But what a waste that would be, Leonie Marshal.'

'You don't have to beat up on me,' she said, aggrieved. 'What do you think you're doing?'

'Some day,' he threatened, 'I'm going to be free of all this mess, and when I do, lady, you just watch out.' He turned away from her. She ducked down and snatched up two handfuls of snow.

'Mr Wheeler?'

He turned around to face her. With all the energy she could muster she shoved the snow into his face. Cecilia broke out laughing. Leonie turned and ran for her life.

The dinner was humdrum. Steak and potatoes, with a tossed salad on the side. Carol Wheeler joined them at table, dressed in a beautiful form-fitting three-quarter-length Eduarda design, and her hair put up for the occasion. The azure dress was spangled from waist to hem, and sparkled in the light of the chandelier. She sparkled too.

Charlie Wheeler had gone the whole hog as well with white dinner-jacket and black tie. He had shaved just before the meal. His cheeks looked baby-smooth, and his aftershave lotion competed valiantly with Carol's Tron d'Amore perfume.

Aunt Agnes, Cecilia, and Leonie were also at the table, looking like neat but shabby poor relatives. And I don't care, Leonie told herself. I just don't give a damn! There. I didn't *say* it but I did *think* it. There are plenty of other men in Fairview. Well, perhaps not exactly *plenty* but enough. And I'm going to get me one. I wonder where Jeff is these days?

There was conversation during the meal. Cecilia, whose red cheeks had turned her into something as cute as a button, was excitedly telling her mother about their experience shovelling snow. The child was laughing. Her father was smiling. Aunt Agnes grinned from time to time. For some reason Carol was not amused. She yawned a time or two, covering her mouth with a couple of fingers.

'Carol, you're tired?' Charlie was all sympathy.

'A little,' she admitted. 'Is my car ready to go?'

'No, but we have a vehicle or two here if you want to go. I'm afraid the Cadillac will be in the shop for several days.'

'You really can't go,' Aunt Agnes said. 'Dr Jonas said two or three days. And being excessively sleepy is a sign of a minor concussion.'

'Oh, pooh,' Carol trilled. 'I have to be on my way. What would a back-country doctor know about such things?'

'More than you think,' Leonie said. 'He was chief of neurosurgery at Johns Hopkins for thirty years before he came home to retire.'

'I think you ought to stay for at least another day,' Charlie said. 'Then I'll rent you a Porsche and you can go back to——?'

'Framingham,' she said, filling in the blanks. 'A suburb of Boston. I have a condo there, next door to our business offices. And if you think I ought, Charles, then I'll stay. It's rather quaint here. I haven't stayed in a boarding house in all my life.'

'It's not exactly a boarding house,' Aunt Agnes said. 'It's a bed-and-breakfast establishment.'

'And you're serving dinner?'

'Entirely to meet Charlie's needs,' the older woman returned.

'I tell you what,' Carol said, giving them all a big smile. 'Why don't you come back down to Framingham with me, Charlie? It's a small town, but I have a coterie of friends that would amuse you no end. You'll enjoy it immensely. And who knows what it might lead to?'

'As you say, who knows?' Charlie replied.

'I don't wanna go,' Cecilia objected. 'I like it here. The air is cleaner. The people are nicer. I wanna stay here!'

'Cecilia.' Her father said just the one word. His face had turned to granite.

'I don't care. I don't wanna go,' the child said.

Her mother leaned over in her direction. The child pushed back her chair from the table. 'In that case, my dear, we can probably arrange for you to stay here. I'm sure Ms Stone could use the income. You could board here——' Every one of the adults in the room could hear the unsaid remainder: and be out of my way!

'God, I hate you,' the child screamed, and ran from the room. Leonie pushed her chair back, preparing to follow.

Charlie held up his hand. 'Give her a little time to think things over,' he said. 'And as for you, Carol, let's get you back to bed. The more you rest, the better you'll be in the morning.' He solicitously helped her up, and held her arm as he walked her back into the parlour. This time the door closed all the way, with a very firm bang.

Leonie rested both elbows on the table, something that her grandmother would never have allowed, and looked at Aunt Agnes bleakly. 'And outside of that, Mrs Lincoln,' she quoted from an ancient and hoary joke, 'how did you enjoy the theatre?'

Aunt Agnes returned the look. 'We'd do better with Sherlock Holmes,' she commented. 'The game's afoot, my dear. Only I don't know which game it is, or what the rules are.'

'I don't care,' Leonie said, not meaning a single syllable. 'You just watch. By tomorrow afternoon they'll be all snuggy, and the day after the pair of them will be off to—to wherever that place is.'

'Framingham,' the old lady supplied. 'I used to know a boy from Framingham.' There was one piece of celery left in the dish. She picked it out and began to nibble on one end. 'Edgar Wilston. A nice boy. Harvard graduate. We almost—but then there was the war, you know. The Second Great War. He was killed at Guadalcanal.'

'I didn't know,' Leonie said sympathetically.

'No reason why you should,' Aunt Agnes replied. She shook herself, as if shrugging off all the old memories. 'But you'd better hope that Charlie doesn't go with her.'

'Why so?'

'Because every cent we have coming in is from Charlie Wheeler. The bed-and-breakfast bit is a laugher. He's paying full hotel rates. The rent for the barn is astronomical. He pays extra for us to baby-sit the girl. He's still paying off for that schoolroom furniture. As if it were made of gold, that stuff, and he set the rates for all these services himself.' The old lady took an extra-large bite of the celery, and for a moment the only sound in the room came from her munching.

'I—didn't know,' Leonie said in a half-whisper.

The clock in the hall struck eight.

'Maybe you ought to look over the accounts,' Aunt Agnes suggested. 'You've never wanted to do that before, but maybe this is the time.'

'Maybe it is, dear. I've been dodging the knowing for a long time, haven't I? Maybe it's time I grew up and faced the real world. He can't possibly be using that schoolroom furniture. When I stopped down there the other day they had all new stuff.'

'He's not even using the schoolrooms any more,' her aunt added. 'He's taken over all the top three floors of the DeMello building for his staff.'

'What in the world is he up to?' Leonie murmured.

'I thought I knew, love, but this bit with his wife——'

'Former wife,' Leonie said fiercely. 'Former wife.'

'Yes, well, she doesn't seem all that *former* from where I sit.' The old lady got up and headed for the stairs. 'I'll get those accounts for you to look at.'

'Right after I do all these dishes.'

'I can't hardly believe it,' she told herself a while later as she looked at the final figures in the account book. She was hunched up in one of the captain's chairs by the kitchen table, with only the light of a single floor lamp to cut through the darkness.

'You can't hardly believe what?' The male voice behind her, out of the darkness, startled her. She pushed her chair back and had both feet in running position before his hand on her shoulder restrained her.

'Can't hardly believe what?' he repeated.

'This.' Leonie gestured at the account books spread out in front of her. 'Why, we're practically your pensioners. If I had known that I would have——'

The other hand came down on her other shoulder, not locking her in position, but rather just steadying her from flight. 'Would have what, Leonie?'

'I would have taken that job as a door-to-door salesperson.'

'You would never have been happy at that, girl.'

'I'm not a *girl*. I'm twenty-seven years old, damn you. And what makes you think that I'm happy the way things are now?'

'You were happy here yesterday. What makes you unhappy now?'

'You, damn your eyes. Just what game are you playing with me, Charlie Wheeler?'

'Game?'

'You'd better believe it. What are you up to with that— former wife of yours?'

'I can tell you wouldn't believe me if I told you.'

'Take a chance. Tell me.'

'Not until—not now.'

'You can't have this thing two ways, Charlie. You can't play the game with me and then with Carol too.'

'Oh, I don't intend to do that.'

'Then you'd better just——'

'Shh. You'll wake Carol up—and I've spent a lot of time tonight getting her to sleep.'

'Well, why didn't you just climb into bed with her and satisfy you both?'

'Yeah. That would. Satisfy us, of course.' He looked down at her, but with only the lamp turned on she missed the look on his face, and didn't hear the nuances in his voice. 'Only you've got to remember she's a possible concussion patient. What do you think the doctor would have to say if we—if Carol and I did, and she had a relapse?'

'Oh? Now you're worried about your reputation?'

He pulled her chair out from the table, and then her out of the chair, standing her at attention. She was so close to him that the tips of her shoes were touching the tips of his. Leonie took a deep breath and held it. There was a rage, a fear running through her, and her besieged mind could not separate the two. Nor could it explain them.

'I'm not worried about my reputation,' he said. 'You've got to understand. I was married to Carol for several years. I haven't been able to drop the feeling of responsibility until——' He stopped talking.

'Until what?'

His hands were on her shoulders again, pulling her towards him. The tips of her breasts brushed against his chest, and a spurt of fire ran up her spine. She struggled against the mental compulsion, and managed to lean back an inch or two.

'So if you feel that strongly towards Carol,' she said, 'just why are you doing all this to me?'

'You don't think I could handle two women at the same time?'

'I don't believe in polygamy. Turn me loose.'

'Yes. In just a minute.' This time he pulled her towards him with more force. She bounced off his chest and then was completely captured. Leonie turned her head, and found her ear over his heart. The powerful throb of it was soporific. All her muscles relaxed.

He pushed her away from himself and that exploring finger came down beneath her chin. It doesn't take long for a girl to learn, she told herself as the dark shadow of his head came down, and his lips touched her gently.

Nothing passionate, just a warm, comforting joining that he broke off quickly.

'Now do me a favour,' he said. 'Don't ask any more questions. In twenty-four hours everything will turn out all right. Just go to bed, lady. Have a nice dream.'

He turned her towards the stairs and gave her a gentle pat on her posterior. She walked over to the foot of the stairs, put her hand on the banister, and then stopped and turned back in his direction. She was tired, and her brain was rattling around inside her skull like a bean in a gourd. 'Just twenty-four hours? Then you're really going to Framingham with her? Lord, you are some rotten sort of guy, Charlie Wheeler!'

With which she slipped out of her shoes and ran up the stairs as if the house were haunted, and all the ghosts were after her.

CHAPTER NINE

LEONIE began on one of her favourite foods, Puerto Rican *arroz con pollo*—chicken and rice, with lots of other things mixed in. The chicken was simmering gently, while the rice and capers waited their turn. Puerto Rican Irish stew, her grandmother had always called it. It had suffered through many Yankee modifications.

The sun peeked brilliantly through the windows, and the snow was beginning to melt. Despite all the pleasures of sun and snow and cooking odours, Leonie was still down at the mouth. The house was quiet. Even Tighe, a magnificent snorer, was sleeping quietly in the corner. Then the back door opened.

'Hello, the house!'

Leonie, who was sampling the sauce with her big wooden spoon, spilled a few hot drops on her chin and dropped the spoon into the mixture. 'Dr Jonas!' She rushed over to help the little old man out of his coat and scarf. 'How did you get out here?'

'The roads are all ploughed in this direction,' he said. 'Not downtown, but everything going north.'

'But the drive——'

'There's some big bohunk out there with a shovel and a big smile. Looks big enough to huff and puff and blow the snow away without a shovel. Just your size, Leonie.'

'Just my——'

'That's right, girl. Can't be single all your life just because some no-good came by and ran a con game on you. Just your size. And pleasant as the day is long.'

'You should know him a little bit longer,' she grumbled.

'Name's Wheeler,' he said. 'Any relation to the patient?'

'Her husband—well, her divorced husband.'

'Well, now,' the doctor said as he dropped into a chair. 'You almost gave me palpitations. I'm never wrong, you know.'

'About what?'

'Romance, child, romance. I'm a great one for seeing good matrimonial matches.'

The sauce bubbled. Leonie went back to give it another stir. 'You've never missed?'

'Not once. Where's the patient?'

Still stirring, Leonie looked up at the clock. 'Eight o'clock? I'm not sure the patient's awake, Doc. She comes from Framingham.'

'Ah. That explains it. The closer people get to Boston, the more—the later they get up. And like that.'

Leonie put her spoon away and smiled at him. It was easy to do. He had the round-faced look of one of Santa's smaller assistants, including a bald head fringed with a straggly bit of white hair. Behind his glasses rested a brain of enormous capacity, limited only by his arthritic frame.

'Hit the wall, did she?'

'Yes. I understand that she was trying to make the turn into the drive when she came across a patch of ice and slid into the wall. The car——'

'Gone, love. Towed away. The town garage is going to make a fortune this month. Lots of business. What was she doing out in that storm? Even the Bostonians knew to stay inside.'

'I—I don't know. It must have been something urgent.'

'Or she must have been three sheets to the windward. Find a bottle in the car, did you?'

'I—didn't look. He—Mr Wheeler—did all the handling. All I got to do was call the garage, and shovel a little snow. You'd have to ask—Mr Wheeler.' Her tongue had stuck on the Charlie. Mr Wheeler he would have to be through this one day, and then surely he'd be gone. Why else would he be up so early, shovelling snow?

'He's coming in in just a minute,' the doctor said. 'Had the path shovelled all the way down to the dirt. You don't see shovelling like that these days. Man to be admired. Now if I had a cup of coffee——'

At least that's something I can do, Leonie told herself as she went over to the stove where the percolator sat, its little red light gleaming. Now if I could only find a man like Dr Jonas. Oh, forty years younger, of course, and maybe a little taller.

But whoa up, lady, that's a prescription for Jeff Littler. But Jeff was all nicety on the outside and villainy on the inside. Gone to warmer climes, had Jeff. Cedar Junction, the state's only maximum-security prison. No little old ladies to be fleeced. No Leonie Marshals to be bamboozled.

She was so engrossed in her memories that she burned the tip of her finger as she brought the hot mug over to the table. In the presence of fine people like the doctor, ladies didn't swear. So Leonie did her best to mutter under her breath. It didn't help. He was wearing his hearing aid, and laughed. And then Charlie Wheeler came in.

'Ah. Dr——'

'Jonas.' Leonie filled in the blank, her heart swelling just from the looking at him. He was wearing a Fair Isle sweater and padded trousers. And a big smile which came from being out in the fresh air. There was a fine sprinkling of snow, rapidly melting, in his black hair.

'Dr Jonas,' he repeated. 'Good of you to come out in this mess.'

'No mess at all,' the doctor said as he sipped his coffee. 'It's our usual weather. A little early, to be sure, but usual. Have you had your coffee? Leonie is the best coffee-maker in the district. Best cook too, for a fact.'

'Dr Jonas!' Leonie was wearing a blush more colourful than the Russian flag.

'Needs to be said,' the doctor commented. 'Give the man a cup of coffee.'

Leonie went to obey. But when she grounded a second mug down in front of Wheeler she could not restrain herself. 'I am not,' she said, 'up on the block at the slave auction!'

'You are also,' the doctor returned, 'not yet married.'

'There's something to be said about old-fashioned customs,' Charlie Wheeler said as he toasted her with his mug—and promptly burned his tongue.

Serves you right, Leonie Marshal thought as he sat there gasping. Damned self-centred, masochistic man! Unfortunately, as she remembered too late, he had this fantastic ability to read her mind.

'Don't think things like that, Leonie.' She was standing too close to him to escape retribution. One of his hands trapped her chin, transferring the chill from his palm to her face. And then, to make things worse, he pulled her down to his level and very thoroughly kissed her. She came up gasping. He came up with a certain gleam in his eye, most readily translated, even by a woman of Leonie's limited experience.

'Yes, well,' the doctor interrupted. 'May I see my patient?'

Standing up for her sisterhood, Leonie said, 'Not this minute. I'll go in and wake her up and——'

'I've seen more women awakened unwarned than you know, Leonie Marshal.' The doctor grounded his mug and pushed himself away from the table.

'And I've been married to this woman for a couple of years,' Charlie Wheeler added. 'C'mon, Doc.' The pair of them left the kitchen, heading for the door of the parlour. Not knowing what else to do, Leonie tagged along.

It was as she had expected. Carol Wheeler was a restless sleeper. She was sprawled all over the extra-wide sofa, one of her feet out from under the sheets, and her nightgown hiked way up to here. She came awake with a shriek, only suppressed when she recognised Charlie.

There was a quick reorganisation. She seemed to be able to shift her face around, to reach the placid expression that restored a part of her beauty. But only a part, Leonie noticed. Without any make-up the little wrinkles around her eyes were as visible as the Martian canals. And, unable to hold her head up, the shadow of a double chin was plain. If it were I, Leonie thought, I'd kill them both!

But the doctor was not impressed. 'More light,' he commanded. Leonie scurried over to the windows and raised the blinds.

'Do you have to?' Carol Wheeler moaned.

'I have to,' the doctor said. He opened his medical bag, took out the necessary instruments, thumbed back Carol's eyelid, and directed the little light directly in. Whatever he was looking for he didn't find. The light moved to the bump on Carol's forehead. 'Hmmph,' the doctor said.

A thermometer appeared in his hand, and disappeared into Carol's mouth. She mumbled a word or two and then was silent. Moments later he took it out, walked over to the brightness of the window space to read it, and then thoughtfully came back. His fingers dived into the mass of Carol's hair and felt around for something. 'Any place hurt?'

'No—not at the moment,' Carol said as she looked around cautiously at Charlie.

'Good,' Dr Jonas said. 'No concussion. You can go back to Framingham today if you want. Relax for a couple of days. Stay in bed. No alcohol. Two aspirins every eight hours. See your local man. You don't need a prescription.' With that the little old man packed up his bag and headed for the kitchen. Leonie followed him, and Charlie was not far behind.

'Got another stop. Baby,' the doctor said. 'I could stand another mug of coffee first.' Leonie complied. 'Only thing still working the way it used to,' the doctor commented. 'Babies. They come when they're ready.'

'But what about——?' Charlie began.

'Your wife?' The doctor tapped his forefinger on the table as he thought. 'Nothing wrong with your wife, young man. There might have been a little shock involved, but I suspect—to be frank, I don't believe there ever was anything wrong with her. God still looks after fools and drunkards. Does your wife drink?'

'She still drinks,' Charlie admitted. 'And she's not my wife. Divorced, you know.'

'I know. A little bird told me.' The little doctor pushed his chair back. 'And now, Spinster Marshal, a trip to your bathroom and I'll be off to catch up to that baby.' He knew his way around the house, and needed no guidance.

'Spinster?' Charlie Wheeler asked as the doctor disappeared. 'A little bird told him?'

'A great kidder, the doctor,' Leonie said as she began to pick up the coffee-mugs. 'And I don't know any talking birds. May I ask what your plans are? Will you be here for supper?'

'Hey, I'm not finished with that.' He caught her hand as she tried to pick up his mug. She sighed, and returned it to him. 'Yes, I'll be here for supper. And Cecilia will too. My girl thinks a lot of you.'

'Not me, my cooking,' Leonie said bitterly. 'Cupboard love.'

'Any kind of love is all right with me,' he said as he got up and reached for his heavy sweater.

'Charles, I need you.' The call came from the parlour. It could be heard all around the house.

'Me too,' he muttered. 'I've got to shovel down to the barn. We may need a car before the day is out.' He disappeared through the kitchen door, and out into the snow.

'Crazy,' Leonie muttered as she rescued the dirty coffee-mugs and set them to soak in the sink. 'The whole family is crazy.' Her big wooden spoon was lying on the sideboard, as if reminding her of something. She picked it up and began stirring, thus missing the grand entrance as Carol Wheeler came out to the kitchen, still buttoning her robe over her diaphanous nightgown.

'Where's Charlie?' the woman demanded as she pulled a chair out from the table and thumped it down.

'Out shovelling.'

Carol rushed to the window and pulled back the curtains. 'I can't see him. Go out and get him for me.'

'Who, me? Look lady, I don't do windows and I don't do messenger service. As it happens I'm not the servant around here, I'm the owner.'

'I need him,' the blonde said desperately. 'I can't go out like this. I've been ill, you know.'

'Yes, I know,' Leonie returned. 'Despite the doctor's opinion. If *you* want him, *you* get him.'

The woman sighed gustily. 'And that's another thing I want to talk to you about.'

And here we go, Leonie told herself. This is where we get down to the nitty-gritty. Like, for instance, Why are you fooling around with my husband? But instead of saying all that she merely said, 'So talk. Did you want breakfast?'

'Sit down and talk to me, eyeball to eyeball,' the blonde insisted.

Leonie shrugged and joined the woman at the table. 'And now?'

'There's too much loose living in this house,' Mrs Wheeler said, clearing the space for battle. 'And Charles is mine. Lock, stock and barrel, he's mine for as long as I want him. And I want him now. In the meantime I'll thank you to take your country-miss claws out of him. Go try your hand at some of the local men.'

'That's about the best advice I've heard in years,' Leonie said. 'But I'm not trying to seduce your husband. He's trying to seduce me—I think. Maybe you ought to tell him what the ground rules are?'

The blonde Mrs Wheeler burst out into raucous laughter. 'Seduction? I wouldn't mind that in the least, Ms——'

'Marshal.'

'Yes, Ms Marshal. I don't mind if you want to have the wildest fling in the world with Charles. He's still mine, but I don't intend to tie him to my apron strings. That was the mistake I made last time. Is that clear?'

'It couldn't hardly be any clearer, lady. Do you really have an apron?'

'I—don't be snippety, young lady. Everyone has an apron. I've got one or two around my kitchen, I'm sure. Keep your hands off my husband.'

'Yes. Well said.' Leonie leaned back in her chair. Her comments evidently astonished the other woman.

'You don't—care?'

'Oh, I care about Charlie, but then, he's taken, isn't he?' The blonde nodded. 'Anyway, as an affair it didn't get very far.' And next year, Leonie told herself, I'm going to apply to Liars Anonymous for a lifetime membership.

'After all,' she told the woman across the table from her, 'it was only twice. A double one-night stand, you might say. Hardly worth all the bother, don't you think?'

'Ah, I knew it! When was the last time?'

'About four hours ago,' Leonie said prettily. 'I don't know how you got it out of me. He likes those morning-hour shots, doesn't he?'

There was no answer from across the table. Carol Wheeler, who tried to give the impression that she was a real swinger, had got up from the table and disappeared into her makeshift bedroom, slamming the door behind her.

Leonie sighed. 'Oh, no,' she said. That door had always been a problem, ever since Grandpa Marshal had rehung it some sixty years ago!

'Did I miss my mother?' Cecilia came down the stairs. Tighe got up from his corner and came over to the foot of the stairs to meet her.

'You missed her.'

'Well, there's always another day.' The child seemed not the least bit concerned. 'And the doctor came? I heard voices. Lucky it was the doctor. My dad is a very—intense sort of man.'

'You mean he's jealous as hell?'

'Now that's what I like about you. Straight to the point. But I didn't think you knew.'

'I didn't. I still don't. Your mother's probably going to leave some time today. You might want to say goodbye?'

'It'll wait,' Cecilia said. 'What's for breakfast?'

'You know what I like about you?'

'No, what? Yes, I'll have orange juice this morning. What *do* you like about me?'

'Everything,' Leonie said as she poured the juice. 'You're just the sort of daughter I would like to have around.'

'Yeah, I can see that.' The child favoured her with a little smile. My lord, she's beautiful, Leonie thought.

'And though I usually don't like other women in my family,' the child said, 'I could stand having you around the house a whole lot.'

They beamed at each other. And the house reverberated as someone with more muscle than wit pounded on a door.

'Your mother, I believe,' Leonie said. 'I wish she wouldn't have slammed that door. I just knew there'd be trouble.'

'You gonna do something about it?'

'I suppose I should,' Leonie replied. 'But not just yet. First I get you your breakfast. What would you like?'

'Blueberry pancakes?'

'Not entirely impossible, young lady. I can hear Aunt Agnes stirring around upstairs. Blueberry pancakes coming up.'

'And Aunt Agnes coming down,' the old lady announced as she came down the stairs. 'What's for breakfast?'

'Blueberry pancakes,' Leonie announced. Her busy hands were dealing with the ingredients.

'Sounds great,' a deep masculine voice commented. Leonie turned around and blushed. Cut that out, she told herself angrily. Why bow to the man? His head is already too big for his hat. Charlie, struggling with his heavy sweater, winked at her.

'I'll get the plates,' Cecilia announced. Her father stared at her as if she had developed horns on her head. Leonie, looking over her shoulder, smiled at the action. And if I plan a family, she thought, I'll choose a man like him. But why dream? She gave herself a mental shake, and paid a little more attention to the pancakes.

The first round lasted barely five minutes. Leonie picked up the antique platter and refilled it.

'Don't you hear something banging?' Aunt Agnes asked.

'Not me,' Leonie said. What the hey? If you're in for a penny...isn't that the way the old saying goes?

'Me neither,' Cecilia commented. 'Must be the wind.'

'There isn't any wind today,' her father objected. He turned his head and listened. 'Good lord, what have you people done with my—with Carol?'

'Nothing yet,' Leonie said frigidly. 'Just give me a few minutes.'

'You've locked her in the parlour?'

'There's no lock on that door,' Aunt Agnes observed.

'But we always have trouble with it when somebody slams it shut,' Leonie reported.

'And nothing is to be done by any of you?'

'Not true,' Leonie said. 'I plan to sit down here and eat my breakfast.'

'Damn.' He pushed his chair back and started for the parlour door, which was being rattled as if an elephant were trapped inside.

'Then you don't mind if I finish your pancakes?' his daughter enquired. Her father paid her no attention. She picked up his plate and slid all its contents on to her own. Her father banged on the door without success, then moved a few inches away from the door and gave it a massive kick. The door groaned, but did not budge. Another kick. A scream from inside, and a third kick. This time the door broke loose from whatever had been jamming it, and swung open—violently, to equal the violence of its closing. And it carried Carol Wheeler, who had been at the keyhole, all the way across the room and on to the couch.

'Charles! Thank God it's you. These people have kept me locked in this room for hours! And you know how claustrophobic I get when I'm locked in somewhere.'

'I know, Carol.' He held out his arms; she fought her way clear of the couch, and he enveloped her.

'I don't want to see this,' Leonie said. She put down her spatula and walked over to the kitchen windows, out of the line of sight. Her heart was heavy in her body, her spirits about as low as one could get in a living human being.

'Don't,' Aunt Agnes murmured.

'Don't what?'

'Don't let yourself believe that it's all over, child.'

'Yeah, chin up,' Leonie said mournfully. 'Look at me smile.' There wasn't a trace of a smile on her heart-shaped face. If this were disaster, she told herself, it would be Disaster ten, Leonie nil. This has to be the positive bottom in my life! But, of course, that wasn't quite true.

Charlie Wheeler came out of the parlour with his former wife on his arm. Former hell, Leonie snorted. The pair of them had just got more than each deserved.

'Sit here.' Charlie pulled out a chair next to Cecilia. As soon as her mother was seated the child, with great deliberation, got up and moved to the other side of the table.

'I suppose none of you can explain why my—Carol—was locked in the parlour?'

'That makes a nice metaphysical dilemma,' Aunt Agnes said. 'There aren't any locks on the parlour door, and haven't been in all the years I've lived in this house.'

'Then explain,' he rumbled, staring straight at Leonie. She shrugged her shoulders and gave him that 'why me?' look. He continued to watch her, and in the watching was a terrible commandment to answer. 'The door is warped,' Leonie said. 'When you bang it shut it has the tendency to stick. The warping was caused by the weather and an amateur carpenter. Since the carpenter is long dead, and the weather is under God's control, I suppose He meant for all this to happen.'

For just a second Leonie would have sworn he smiled. But only for a second, and, since they were sitting around the table in such a fashion that his back was to the windows and the sun was shining directly into her eyes, perhaps the whole darn thing was an optical mirage.

In any event Carol was having none of it. 'Somebody locked me in,' she insisted. 'I've got to get out of this place before something more drastic happens to me. Charles?'

'Yes, my dear. I can have the Jeep at the door in fifteen minutes or so. Why don't you go pack, and we'll be off? Would you like some breakfast before we go?'

'I wouldn't dare eat a morsel prepared in this house,' Carol said firmly.

'That's not a morsel, that's *arroz con pollo,*' Cecilia retorted. Her accent was terrible, but was about as close to the correct Spanish as the stew was to the original recipe. The girl got up, walked around the table to kiss Leonie, and ran for the stairs.

'Cecilia,' her father roared, but the girl was already out of sight, pounding up the stairs. 'Like a herd of wild animals,' her father said, sighing. 'Is it always going to be like this?'

'It gets worse when they get to adolescence,' Aunt Agnes commented. 'You'll love it, you and your—wife. I'd give the child about four more years before she becomes a real hellion.'

'There. See?' Carol pushed back her chair and raced towards the parlour.

'Don't slam the door,' Leonie called after her. She was rewarded by a massive slamming. Leonie looked over at Charlie and shrugged.

'You don't understand,' he said in a strained voice. 'It'll all work out in the end. My—Carol—is a sensitive woman in a man's world. She's been running the other parts of the Wheeler grocery chain, and has run into a lot of trouble.'

'Nothing she can handle?' The moment she said it, Leonie felt embarrassed. 'I mean—nothing she can't——'

'I know what you mean,' he interrupted. 'You don't like Carol very much, do you?'

'Is it obligatory that I like her? This is only a bed-and-breakfast lease, not a convention of Holy Church.'

'Don't,' he said, suddenly soft and loving. 'It doesn't fit your character, Leonie Marshal. The poor woman came running to me because they're trying to push her into bankruptcy. Since Cecilia and I are still minority stockholders in both companies, she felt she had to have a release signed by me to be on safe ground.'

'And of course you signed?'

'Of course.'

'Just to protect Carol's and Cecilia's rights?'

'Correct.'

'But then you're long past the deadline. There hasn't been any mail moved since just before the storm. A total waste of time, then, all this?'

'Not exactly. You did know that I have a computer up in my bedroom?'

Leonie nodded. There didn't seem to be *anything* in the electronic world that he didn't have some part or connection with.

'And then you might not know that I have a telephone modem up there? And a connection to your telephone?'

'Interesting,' Aunt Agnes commented. 'I'd love to see how it all works. So you faxed the agreement, and everything is all right for her?'

'Not quite,' he said enigmatically. 'Everything's all right for the moment, but I'm not the soft-hearted fool you think me, Leonie Marshal. Sooner or later Carol's whole house of cards is going to collapse. And when it does she'll want us to remarry. Isn't that a laugh?'

He snatched up his heavy outdoor sweater and made for the door. 'Cecilia?' No answer from upstairs. He shook his head in disgust and opened the kitchen door. A cold wind bustled in. Leonie shivered.

'So how do you know that whoever pressured her towards bankruptcy wouldn't try it again?' she called after him.

'Oh, I'll know,' he said, chuckling. 'The villain of the piece is my grandfather! Look after Cecilia for me, will you?'

'Yeah, take care of Cecilia,' Leonie muttered. 'Mustn't let the beautiful Carol be held down by a daughter, A nine-year-old daughter. Funny how having a child dates one.'

'You'd like to have one of your own, wouldn't you?' Aunt Agnes said. 'Wouldn't it be nice to have one or two little people around the house?'

'If I had known you felt that way,' Leonie grumbled, 'I would have hired a couple of the Little People when the circus came by this summer.'

'Leonie Marshal,' her aunt lectured, 'don't think you can pull the wool over *my* eyes. You're just like my favourite candy bar—hard chocolate on the outside and marshmallow in the middle. Now go find the girl. Her father won't want to wait for her.'

'I'm going, I'm going.' Leonie collected the dirty dishes and left them to soak in the sink, and then started for the stairs.

'Don't bother,' Carol Wheeler said.

'I—how did you get out of the parlour?' Leonie gasped.

The blonde was standing in the archway that led to the dining-room. She was fully clothed, including gloves and hat. Not a hat that would be of any use in a storm or on a farm, but a perky little thing that might have caught some man's eye. 'I didn't come down in yesterday's snow storm,' Carol said. 'That was the closet door that I slammed.' She came further into the kitchen. Her unblemished face was made up to perfection. 'Now if you will kindly move my luggage out to the vehicle, I'll be on my way.'

Aunt Agnes said bitterly, 'Leonie is not a servant in this house.'

'You surely don't expect me to carry all that? I'm not a well woman, you know.'

'That's not what the doctor said.' Aunt Agnes had battle lights in her eyes. Leonie put a restraining hand on her shoulder, and was shaken off.

'No. Don't argue, Aunt Agnes. It's not worth it. I'd be glad to carry all her bags to the street if it would get her out of my house sooner. And where, *madame*, would you like me to send you the bill for your stay in our establishment?'

Carol sneered at them both and resettled her stole around her neck. 'My husband takes care of that sort of thing,' she said haughtily. 'Can you imagine, Charles Wheeler living in a boarding house?'

Charles Wheeler caught the tail-end of that conversation as he came into the house, blowing on his chilled hands. 'And enjoying every minute of it,' he said. 'Are we ready to go?'

'I am, but these—incompetents—seem to have lost my daughter. Our daughter,' she hastened to correct. 'The more I think of it, the more I like the idea of leaving Cecilia here, Charles. She would hardly fit into the society with which I mingle in the Boston area.'

Charlie Wheeler nodded. 'Perhaps a good idea. Let's get packed up and be on our way. If Cecilia shows up, well and good. If not——' He shrugged his shoulders as he looked at Leonie. 'You *will* take care of her until I come back, Leonie?'

'What a rotten thing to say, Charlie Wheeler. Going off and abandoning your daughter just so you——'

'But you *will* take care of her?'

'Of course I will. Just get out of my house, you——'

'Leonie!'

'I can't help it, Aunt Agnes. This is about the most heartless pair of parents I've ever met.' It was hard to hide the tears, but she managed—just.

'Yes, well, I plan to do something about that,' Charlie Wheeler said. There was a distant chilling quality in his voice, as if he were already fifty miles away. Silence enveloped the foursome. A thick palpable silence that hung over everyone like a mad indoor cloud, prepared to rain.

'I'll get your bags,' Charlie finally said. And in moments he was back, loaded with luggage. In a few more minutes everything was stored in the Cherokee, and without further ado the Wheelers fled up the drive and out on to the county highway.

Leonie, standing by the window, watched them as they chafed each other and drove away. 'So that's that,' she said mournfully.

'That's what, child?'

'He's gone. I'll bet you a buck against a Canadian ten-cent piece that they never come back. Neither one of them.'

'Oh, they'll be back,' her aunt assured her. 'He will, anyway.'

'Have they really gone?' asked Cecilia, creeping down the stairs in her stocking feet.

'They've gone,' Leonie said. 'You needn't be surprised. Aunt Agnes and I will be glad to share our home with you. Don't cry.'

'I wasn't going to cry,' the little girl said. 'My dad explained it all to me last night. Why do you keep calling her Aunt Agnes? She's not your for-real aunt, is she?'

'Yes, she's my for-real aunt,' Leonie said firmly. 'We were both lonely, and then we met and adopted each other, and now she's my for-real aunt.'

'That must be wonderful,' the guileless child said. 'Do you suppose I could——?'

'I don't see why not,' Leonie promised. 'If your father is gone for more than seven years he can be presumed dead in Massachusetts, and we—Aunt Agnes and I—would be glad to adopt you.'

'Then that's all right,' the girl said, a smile flashing across her square little face. 'We won't have to wait seven years. He'll be back tomorrow.'

CHAPTER TEN

THE day which had shown so much promise began to fade shortly after mid-morning. The skies darkened as the meteorological service began to issue more storm bulletins. Snow began to spit at the house a little after ten o'clock.

Things were so dark that Leonie turned on the kitchen lights, and then slumped down at the table, her mind a morass. Everything she had thought of had become a self-fulfilling prophecy. Yesterday Charlie Wheeler had gone, along with Carol. Perhaps no longer his *former* wife. And not a word had been heard from him since. So Leonie was hunched over the kitchen table, still in her long white flannel nightgown, wondering why she had got up at all.

'Why so gloomy?' Cecilia asked as she came down, dressed in pyjamas and slippers.

There's no use trying to hide it all, Leonie thought. The child probably feels worse than I do. And with good reason. Abandoned by her father, not loved by her mother. Poor, poor kid.

'I'm sorry, dear. But when your father abandoned you I thought it a terrible thing, and——'

'Abandoned me? You've got rocks in your head, lady!'

'I don't know how you can take it so well,' Leonie continued mournfully. 'But I'm proud that you do. You can be sure that Aunt Agnes and I will do our best to take care of you.'

'That's nice of you, but I don't need taking care of. I can——'

'Taking care of whom?' Aunt Agnes interrupted as she slippered down the stairs and joined them.

'For some crazy reason,' Cecilia said, 'your niece here thinks my father has abandoned me in the wild woods of the west.'

'Crazy? Well, perhaps a little confused,' the old lady replied. 'Now if I could get a couple of cups of coffee under my belt, we might reason this whole thing out.' She came over to the table, pulled out her favourite chair, and sat down.

Leonie moved automatically, filling a mug and bringing it back to the table. 'Cocoa, Cecilia?' she asked. The child nodded and pulled up her own chair. 'And orange juice?' Another nod.

'And another piece or two of that French bread you baked yesterday. If there's any left.'

'There's plenty.' Leonie busied herself in service, watching the two of them as she did so. Three females, she thought. Will it always be this way? Aunt Agnes is getting old, and Cecilia ought to have a couple of siblings around the house. Instead we're all going to hole up here in this old house, and grow older together. Life just isn't fair, is it, Leonie Marshal? She refilled her own mug and joined the other two at the table.

'Now, then, what's this about Cecilia being abandoned?' asked Aunt Agnes.

'You saw the pair of them yesterday,' Leonie muttered. 'Rushing off to Boston and——'

'Framingham,' the little girl interrupted.

'Yes, well, Framingham—and didn't even stop long enough to see if we could find Ceci here. Callous! Lord, the pair of them would make a fine couple of Siberian wolves. Can't you see them chasing the sleigh over the snow, looking to devour——?'

'Leonie, get a grip on yourself. They just went off to Framingham. It's not the end of the world. Anyone could drive that far in three hours or so. Which reminds me, Cecilia, where were you hiding?'

The girl giggled as she stirred her drink. 'Up in the attic. Nobody's been up there in ages, I *betcha*. The whole place is cobwebs and trunks and old furniture. I had a lot of fun. There are some dresses up there that would make you blush, Leonie. I tried one on, and——'

'I don't care about that,' Leonie interrupted—and then sat quietly with her hands folded in her lap.

'Funny thing,' her aunt commented. 'It used to be possible for almost anyone to complete a sentence in this house. Now one can hardly get off a phrase or two before the interruptions start. Cecilia, what about your father?'

'What about him? My dad, he's a very—devious, I think the word is—man. He wanted my mother to go back to Framingham and the quickest way to get that done was to drive her himself. He's doing some kind of business hanky-panky——'

'Devious I could believe,' Leonie muttered. 'But hanky-panky?'

'Do you know something else my dad says?'

'No. What?' Leonie asked.

'He says that for an old lady of twenty-eight——'

'Twenty-seven,' Leonie corrected. 'That's not so old.'

'All right. He says that for an old lady of twenty-seven, Leonie, you're really very, very young. And then he laughed, as if he was glad of that.'

'Thank you very much,' Leonie retorted angrily. 'Such a compliment. Did your dad say anything else of importance?'

'Lots of things, but I don't think you'd want me to tell you. Except for one. When he said he was going to drive Mother back to Framingham he said he'd be back here before noon today, and he was "gonna settle her hash for her". I don't understand what that means. Do you?'

'I have no idea,' Aunt Agnes said. 'Leonie, you'd better make a big dinner for tonight. And how about some of those croissants you used to bake? They'd make a big hit.'

'Croissants?' Leonie sighed. 'I suppose it's possible. Providing we don't have another blizzard. Settle whose hash, do you suppose?'

The other two females present stared at her for so long that she began to feel she had spots on her nose. Nervously she left the table. Surely there was something else that needed doing, she told herself. But what?

'If you really want to know, why don't you ask *him*?' Cecilia said innocently. But her giggle gave her away. And a motor roared as the Cherokee Jeep came storming down the drive and was pulled to a halt just by the back door.

Within seconds Charlie Wheeler bounced up the stairs and into the kitchen, where he stamped his boots a couple of times on the rug, and then threw off his anorak. 'Starting to snow again,' he announced. 'Look at this, will you, my whole harem just waiting for me?'

Three chairs scraped back. 'Daddy,' Cecilia yelled as she jumped at him. He caught her in mid-air and swung her up for a kiss. He looks so tired, Leonie thought. So worn. I had thought we might have fed him up to style, but——

'That's all the kissing I get?' He set his daughter down gently, and patted her bottom.

'Well, I wouldn't mind a sample,' Aunt Agnes said as she limped over to him and offered a cheek. 'Welcome home, Charlie. Leonie? Your turn.'

'I—perhaps——'

'Daddy, Leonie didn't think you was coming back, and she cried all night long, and who is it that you're gonna settle her hash for her?'

'Cried all night, did she? That's interesting news.' His deep voice rolled over Leonie's head and brought comfort in its passing. He held out both arms in her direction.

'Blabbermouth,' she muttered, but was unable to hold her feet still. In fact she fought against their movement, one step at a time, and hadn't the power to make them stop. Until her nose bumped into his chest, that was, and the gates closed behind her.

Vaguely, in the distance, she could hear Aunt Agnes. 'Come on, child, let's you and I get out of the way.'

'But I wanna watch,' Cecilia complained.

'There's a fine television programme on,' Aunt Agnes insisted. '*Bullwinkle and Rocky*. You'll love it.'

'Your aunt is a very sensible woman,' he murmured into her ear. 'Now, then. Cried all night, did you?'

'I thought you weren't coming back,' she admitted.

'Waste of time and tears, wasn't it? Bad pennies, and all that.'

'You've got it just right,' he said, chuckling. 'Want me to leave?'

'Lord, no!'

'Then hush up. Today's the day we settle your hash.'

'Me?'

'You. Sit down. And I could use some hot coffee too.'

Leonie had lived in a manless house for years, but she knew the drill. I don't sit down until I bring him his coffee, she told herself. Damn man! I'm not his servant!

He took a couple of restorative sips, then put both elbows on the table, rested his chin in the palms of his hand, and sighed. 'I'm beat,' he said. 'Really beat.'

'And I suppose you're going to tell me about it.' Leonie sniffed at him and tried to look away.

'None of that now.' He reached over and tilted her chin in his direction, then renewed his stance. 'My former wife has managed to run the rest of the Wheeler grocery chain into the ground.' He took a couple more sips of coffee. 'That takes real skill, let me tell you.'

'Sarcasm doesn't become you,' she told him.

'Yes, you're right. So anyway, since I am still a minority stockholder, she had to get my signature to put the whole outfit into bankruptcy. After my lawyer and I gave her a talking-to, that's what she's about to do.'

'I'm terribly interested,' Leonie said as she yawned in his face.

'Sometimes you're not much fun,' he said as he shook his head. 'Look, she applies to the court for relief under chapter eleven of the code. That means her creditors can't take her over until she's had a chance to reorganise. And *that* means she has to close down some of the stores or sell them off, until she gets what's left of the company back into the profit column.'

'Do I applaud now?'

'That also means that I've left my lawyer instructions to snap up any of the stores that come on the market. For ten cents on the dollar, Leonie, and—presto—I'm back in the grocery business in a big way.'

'Why, you—you schemer!'

'When you play with the big boys you takes your chances,' he said, chuckling. 'Now there's only this problem. Until all this transpires, my former wife is making noises about us remarrying, and that I can't have.'

Leonie's face fell to Grand Canyon depth. 'So you're going to——'

'So I'm going to marry you,' he concluded.

Leonie slid back in her chair, her mind spinning like a top. 'Now let me understand this,' she said. 'I'm going to marry you to keep your former wife from marrying you? And to take charge of your daughter? And to get my accounts balanced so I can pay the sewer assessment?'

He nodded at each statement. 'A fine deal. We both come out smelling like roses.'

'I don't quite see it that way,' she snapped at him. 'You're going to get all those goodies and all I'm going to get is a sewer line? It smells, all right, but not of roses.'

'Leonie,' he chided. 'Think again. You get your sewer line and my decrepit old body as well.'

'And that's a bargain?' She pushed her chair back and walked around the table, her mind working overtime.

'And then there's one more thing,' he said casually. 'I love you.'

She stopped in mid-stride, one foot still off the floor. 'You——?'

'I love you, Leonie Marshal.' He pushed his own chair away and came around the table, where he picked her up in his arms and cuddled her close. 'And you?'

'I—when can we get married?' A whisper. She had no idea from whom she was keeping this great secret, but it seemed best to whisper.

He wasn't interested in secrecy.

'Just after noontime,' he told her as he kissed the tip of her nose. 'Mr Pruit, the Justice of the Peace, who lives about four blocks from here, allows that he'll be able to come by at lunchtime and do us up all shipshape and Bristol fashion.'

'But we would need a licence and——'

'In my pocket,' he replied. 'I got it three weeks ago over at the county seat.'

'You what? You got the licence three weeks ago, without even asking me? What sort of a person do you think I am, who would marry you under those conditions?' She beat on his chest with her tiny hands, and with all her strength. He didn't seem impressed, so when her fists began to hurt she stopped.

'You look lovely when your face gets all rosy,' he said cheerfully. 'Now, the only problem is, do you love me?'

He set her down on her feet, but kept her close with a hand on each shoulder. 'Leonie?'

'I'll have to vacuum the living-room,' she responded dreamily. 'It's too messy for a wedding.' And then he kissed her again.

By eleven o'clock, with Aunt Agnes and Cecilia to help, the downstairs part of the house was gleaming. Outside the windows the snow was still spitting, but hardly enough to deter movement.

'Nice,' Aunt Agnes said. 'Is that what you're going to wear?'

'It's my best,' Leonie replied. 'Cecilia?'

'I'll go put on a dress,' the girl said, hoping that somebody would forbid it.

'And socks,' Aunt Agnes prodded. 'And don't make any noise. Your dad is trying to get in an hour or two of sleep. He was up all last night.'

'Like a ghost,' the girl promised, and ran up the stairs sounding like a herd of elephants.

'Just think,' Leonie said. 'We have years of that before us.'

'And maybe more,' Aunt Agnes said. 'Isn't it a grand idea?'

'More noise?'

'More babies.' At which the back doorbell rang, and Leonie rushed off to take her blushing face out of the line of fire. There was a man at the door, with his back to the house, dressed for stormy weather. Mr Pruit, early, Leonie thought as she opened the door and welcomed him in. He walked by her as she hurried to close the door against the cold, and only then did she hear Aunt Agnes moan, 'No! Not you again!'

Leonie whirled around. The man had gone into the dining-room, where the older lady was backing up slowly, almost trapped in a corner. He turned around to face Leonie.

'Oh, my God,' she gasped. 'Jeff Littler!'

'The very same,' he said, smiling. Leonie stopped, hand over her heart. He had been a handsome young man five years ago. Now his face had fallen in, there were scars on both cheeks, and his nose had been re-arranged. He was still big and cruel and dangerous. She could never forget how he had attacked both of them, stolen all the money in the house, and would have raped her had not the milk-collection truck driven up at the gate just in time.

'I just happened to be in the neighbourhood and thought I'd drop in,' he said.

'Why? Haven't you done enough to us already?'

'Why? I just got out of the slammer, and it's cold outside and I'm broke—and I figure you both owed me something. So here I am to collect.'

'There's nothing we have to give you,' Leonie said firmly. 'We're broke. I even had to sell the cows.'

'I noticed that,' he said. 'I'll take whatever you've got, and maybe you could make up the difference in trade.'

'I don't know what you mean,' Leonie said although she knew exactly what he meant. She inched her way around the dining-room table so that she could stand beside Aunt Agnes.

Nervous as she was, she barely noticed that her aunt was as cool as a cucumber. 'What this house needs,' the aunt said, 'is to have a big, strong man around.'

Yes, and we have one, Leonie thought. Her courage began to mount the scale. She flashed her aunt a quick smile, took a deep breath, and screamed as if the world were coming to an end. In seconds Aunt Agnes added her strong contralto.

'Won't help,' Jeff Littler said. 'It's snowing outside. There isn't a car on the road, and nobody home next door.'

From behind them, in the parlour, they could hear the roar of the television set, where Cecilia was still engrossed in the cartoons. Their screams made no difference to the little girl.

But out in the warmest corner of the kitchen the sound awakened Tighe from his dreams. The dog came out of the corner as if he were but a two-year-old, his feet moving ten million miles an hour, although the old body was barely making two. The dog came through the arch at best speed, sized up the situation, and tried to stop. The polished floor defeated him. He slid halfway across the room, ending up under the dinner-table. And from that safe point he began to bark as if he were the terror of the north woods.

'Keep your damn dog away from me,' Littler growled. He dropped into a fighting crouch and whipped a switch-blade knife out of his pocket. 'He comes near me and somebody's gonna get hurt.'

'You can say that again!' Charlie Wheeler, racing down the stairs barefoot, and dressed only in his underwear, popped into the dining-room. 'What the hell is going on here? Who is this guy?'

'Let me introduce you,' Leonie said through chattering teeth. 'This is Jeff Littler, my ex-fiancé, the neighbourhood thief and attempted rapist. He wants all our money—again—and whatever else he can get!'

'Well, we'll have to see what we can do about that,' Charlie said. 'Put the knife away, little boy, or else——'

'Or else what?' Littler retorted. 'I'm gonna cut you up in little pieces, and then I'll take the girl.'

'I'm a peaceful man,' Charlie said, his face lit up with an unholy grin. He took three steps forward, so that only the width of the table separated them, and raised both hands in a boxing stance. Littler moved closer to his own side and waved the knife back and forth.

'The knife,' Leonie gasped. 'He could——'

'I see it,' Charlie replied.

Leonie reached out a hand for courage; Aunt Agnes took it and squeezed gently. 'I have all the faith in the world in Charlie,' her aunt said.

'Me too,' Leonie returned, but her voice quavered and she had to bite her bottom lip to keep from crying.

'It'll only take a minute,' Charlie assured them. He shot his left hand forward in a jab. Littler moved eyes and knife to the threatened side. At which point Charlie swung a round-house right hand that connected with a thud on the side of Littler's chin. The man moved out of his crouch. The thug, looking thunder-struck, tried to move forward across the table, still waving his knife.

Charlie backed off, but that was just the moment that Tighe, sure that the battle was over, came out from under the table, still barking, and landed directly behind Wheeler. Charlie, hearing the animal, was unable to change his direction. As a result he tripped over the dog and landed on the floor, his head bouncing off the leg of the side-table. Littler, at the same time, fell flat on top of the table, dropped his knife, and then slid down on to the floor on the opposite side to Charlie. And Tighe stopped barking.

The door to the parlour, not sticking this time, opened and Cecilia stuck her head out. 'I wish you wouldn't make all that noise,' the girl complained. 'I can hardly hear my programme.'

'Yes,' Aunt Agnes responded. 'Go back to your programme. We'll be quiet.' The door closed.

'This one's stirring,' Leonie said as she kicked at Littler's stomach.

'This one isn't,' Aunt Agnes said as she went around the table and knelt beside Charlie Wheeler.

'Heaven helps those who help themselves,' Leonie misquoted as she dashed for the kitchen. In a moment she was back, carrying her cast-iron frying-pan in one hand. 'I'm scared, Aunty,' she gasped as she skidded to a halt.

'That makes two of us,' her aunt said.

'I've never ever hit anybody before in all my life.'

'If you don't hit him, he'll hit us,' her pragmatic aunt declared.

Jeff Littler took that exact second to groan and start to move. Leonie moved closer. The minute his head showed above the level of the dining-room table she swung her frying-pan. The man collapsed. Leonie dropped the pan on to the table and began to take deep shuddering breaths.

At that same moment Charlie Wheeler opened his eyes and groaned. 'Lord, what happened?'

'You tripped over the dog and bumped your head,' Leonie said. She dropped to his side and lifted that head into her lap.

'Littler?'

'He's still out.'

'Well,' Charlie mused. 'What do you know? I really gave it to him, didn't I?'

Crisis time, Leonie told herself. A man and his pride. My man and his pride. 'Yes,' she said, 'you really gave it to him—didn't he, Aunt Agnes?'

'Yes, you really did,' that worthy replied. 'You're what we've always needed around here.'

'That's always been a problem for me,' he said. 'I was always big for my age. My father used to lecture me day after day that since I was so big I should never pick on smaller people. But all I ever found was smaller people, and nobody ever wanted to pick on me. As a result, except for Littler here, I've only hit one other man in all my life. Made me wonder if I *could*, you know. It's good to know. Help me up. I want to see him.'

Leonie did the best she could, but finally it was his own muscles that triumphed. The frying-pan had disappeared from the table-top, Leonie noticed, and caught the whisker of a smile on her aunt's face.

'Now,' he said, 'we'd better call the police. No, we don't have any police in the town. Then what we need to do——'

'The kitchen closet,' Aunt Agnes suggested. 'It has only one door, and there's a lock on the outside.'

'The very thing,' Charlie agreed. He grabbed both of Littler's legs and towed him across the polished floor into the kitchen. The two women stayed in the dining-room and listened to the crash and bang that followed.

Now that the crisis was past both of the women shivered, moving close to hold each other. 'I can't help it,' Leonie murmured. She took off her glasses and started to cry.

'I've only got one handkerchief,' her aunt said, as if that were something important.

'All right now,' Charlie announced as he came back to the dining-room. 'All properly secured. Only if we haven't anyone to turn him over to, what do we do next?'

'We either call the county sheriff or the state police barracks. I'll do that,' Aunt Agnes said, shrugging. There was no use waiting for the pair of them to do anything more. They were completely absorbed in each other, clinging like lost souls waiting for the rescue boat to come and pick them up.

Tighe, his duty done commendably, ambled back out to the kitchen, and his warm corner rug. The parlour door opened again, and Cecilia came out. 'Is it time for the wedding?' she asked.

'Not quite yet,' Aunt Agnes said. 'But we'd better get dressed for the occasion. We only have another hour before Mr Pruit arrives.'

'Yeah, we'd better,' the little girl said as she looked at her father, still busy with the hugging and kissing bit. 'Daddy,' she called. 'Come on now. You can't get married in your underwear.'

CHAPTER ELEVEN

MR PRUIT arrived at twelve-thirty, a short, thin man with cheeks polished red by the cold weather, and a smile big enough to encompass all of Fairview.

'Love to do this,' he told them all. 'Spend half my life with papers and forms and idiots. Gets so a marriage is the only fun there is.'

He shrugged off his coat with Cecilia's help, and followed Charlie into the dining-room. 'Nice,' he commented. 'Everything shiny and clean. I don't see a lot of that outside my office. Now, let me see. You're Mr Wheeler? Say, you must be the owner of our grocery store. It sure perked up a lot in the past two weeks. And you have the licence?'

'Right here.' Charlie held the document up in front of the Justice, who whipped out a pair of gold-rimmed glasses to read.

'Never had this trouble till last year,' Pruit said. 'On my seventy-fifth birthday my eyes all went to hell—er—excuse me, ladies—to Hades. Now then, hmm. Charles Montgomery Wheeler. That's you.' His glasses slipped and he pushed them back up. 'And Leonie Whitedeer Marshal? Seneca Indian, ma'am?'

'Partly,' Leonie confirmed. 'One-eighth, to be exact.'

'And now we have to have two witnesses, and they are——?' A pause while the adults present counted heads.

'Well, I'm one of them,' Aunt Agnes said. 'Agnes Turnbull Stone.'

And there was a moment of silence, until Charlie said, 'How about my daughter Cecilia? She's big for her age.'

Mr Pruit examined the girl and slowly shook his head. 'Has to be an adult,' he said. 'No adult, no marriage. It's the state law, you know. We could always put it off until next week?'

'No!' Leonie exclaimed, in almost the same breath that Charlie said the same thing.

'Maybe we could go out on the highway and flag down some motorist. Does it matter who this adult is?'

'Law doesn't make any distinction, but I don't think you'd have any luck flagging down a car. Hardly anybody's on the road. They're all scared off by that last storm we had.'

'One adult witness,' Charlie murmured. His prospective bride looked up at him with a devilish gleam in her eye.

'Yes,' she said.

'Mr Pruit,' Charlie said. 'You just get everybody lined up, and I'll be back in a minute with a witness.'

As it happened, it took longer than that, but nobody seemed to mind. Charlie dashed out into the kitchen, unbolted the door to the broom cupboard and reached into it with one hand.

'No, you don't,' Jeff Littler said. 'You don't get me to stand up in front of that Justice feller. Not me.'

'Let me make you an offer you can't refuse,' Charlie Wheeler coaxed. 'Come out to the wedding, and just maybe I might have a good word for you when you come up for trial.'

'And if I don't?'

'And if you don't,' Charlie said, having managed to get a grip on Littler's shirt collar, 'I'll break both your arms and both your legs and swear to the police that you were trying to escape.'

'No, I——' But Charlie's arm was too long, and too strong. He yanked the thug out on to the kitchen floor, pulled him over, kneeling, to the kitchen table, and began to talk to him so softly that the eager audience in the dining-room was unable to hear. In a moment both men came into the dining-room, arm in arm, smiling. Well, perhaps one was smiling a bit more than the other.

'Here we go, Mr Pruit. I make you known to Jeffrey Littler, a citizen of the Commonwealth of Massachusetts, who has volunteered to witness the ceremony.'

'Is that right, Mr Littler? Where do you live?'

'I've lived in Walpole for the past few years,' Littler said cautiously. 'At the moment I'm considering living in this area. I have a room at the hotel downtown.'

'Good, good. Walpole? Isn't that where they have the maximum-security——?'

'The very place,' Charlie interrupted him. 'Could we get on with the ceremony?'

'Of course,' the Justice said. 'Now then, Leonie and Charles, you two stand in the middle here and hold hands. No, Mr Wheeler, you hold Leonie's hand, not Mr Littler's.'

'It's a matter of religion,' Charlie said. 'I have to hold Mr Littler's hand as well, to be sure he doesn't get—carried away by the ceremony. It's not illegal, is it?'

'Not at all.' The little Justice paused to wipe his forehead with a very large ornamental handkerchief. 'Not illegal at all, providing this isn't going to turn out to be one of those—different—weddings. Now, are we ready?'

It's *my* wedding, Leonie told herself. So this is only a civil ceremony, and we can have our church wedding later, but I can't believe what's going on. So, as usual in her times of confusion, Leonie Marshal withdrew into herself.

'Dearly beloved...' Justice Pruit began.

And I'll have a long white gown and a veil instead of this blue dirndl affair, and Aunt Agnes will be in something more modern than her pink caftan, and Cecilia can be the flower girl, and——

'. . . so long as ye both shall live?' Mr Pruit read. Somebody nudged Leonie with an elbow.

'I will,' she said. And then we'll go down to the Bahamas for our honeymoon, and all the nights will be moonlit, and the stars will shine on us for all our days, and he will give up all his bad habits and——

'With this ring I thee wed,' Charles said, and somebody was snatching at Leonie's left hand and trying desperately to push a ring on to her finger, and——

'I will,' Jeffrey Littler said.

'Shut up,' Charlie Wheeler said, 'or I'll fix your face.'

'I now pronounce you man and wife,' Mr Pruit said. 'You may kiss the bride.'

And so he did.

After which his bride said, 'What did you do that for?'

'Because we're married,' Charlie Wheeler said with a great deal of warmth. 'And I do believe I'll do it again.'

'Good idea,' Justice Pruit commented. 'Happy bride and groom.'

'Isn't there something in your book about me?' Cecilia asked. 'Now she's my mother, you know.'

And hear the organ swell, thought Leonie.

Sirens, Charlie thought. The cops are here, thank God. 'And we thank you, Mr Pruit. Can you stay for a libation?'

'No, don't believe I can. A work day, you know. I'm only on my lunch-hour.' The little man stuck out his hand, and Charlie, in order to shake it, hand to turn Jeff Littler loose.

Mr Littler immediately headed for the back door, but before he could open it Tighe was nipping at his heels.

In those precious seconds while Charlie was enthusiastically re-kissing his bride, Jeff Littler was standing
against the kitchen wall, trying to protect himself from
a dog who had last bitten anything some ten years before.
He was rescued by a burly state policeman, who took
one look at him and grinned.

'Jeff Littler,' the policeman said. 'Three house bur-
glaries in five days. You've been busy since you got out
of the slammer. What's he charged with, people?'

Everyone else was busy, so Aunt Agnes came over.
'Breaking and entering,' she listed, 'scaring me to death
with a knife, assaulting dear Mr Wheeler—oh, and
having bad breath.'

'He'll be away for years this time,' the policeman said,
laughing. 'Do I get to kiss the bride?'

'I don't see how,' Mr Pruit answered. 'It looks as if
she'll be all tied up for some time. Now, if I may have
Mr Littler sign this, here where it says "witness".'

'Won't they ever come up for air?' Cecilia asked
plaintively. 'I'd like to kiss the bride myself.'

'You've got years ahead of you for that,' Aunt Agnes
said. 'Not to worry.'

The back door slammed as the police took Littler out
to their car.

'And I'd better be going,' Mr Pruit announced as he
went out to the kitchen and shrugged himself into his
coat. 'No, I've already been paid,' he said, when Aunt
Agnes offered him something. 'A very considerable gra-
tuity, I must say. Bless you all.'

'Charlie! Leonie!' Aunt Agnes called to the entwined
pair. 'Come and say goodbye to Mr Pruit.'

'And thank you,' Leonie called out as she and her
husband walked to the door. The pair of them watched
with the door half-open as Mr Pruit made his way up
the drive to his car. The snow was beginning to resemble

a real storm. The cold wind began to eddy around their feet. They both waved, and then Charlie closed and locked the door.

'Look at you,' Charlie Wheeler said softly. 'My little snow bride. What'll we do now?'

'Shovel?' she suggested impudently.

'I've got a better idea.' He picked her up in his arms, both of them laughing, and headed for the stairs. Leonie cuddled up against his chest. And now it's done, she told herself, and I can hear the angels sing. Leonie's luck has suddenly turned all to the good, lady. He whirled them down the hall and kicked the door to his room open. Tighe, who had followed close behind, slipped by and went over to the far corner.

He set Leonie down on her feet, so close that her breasts were touching his chest. 'I hope,' she murmured, 'that you know what we're going to do now, because I don't.'

'A farm girl, and you don't know what we're going to do?'

'Well, I know the theory, but not the practice, you see.'

'How lucky can I get?' he said, chuckling. 'All the way out in the country and I've found a real virgin?' His hands were busy. Leonie could feel a cold draught coming from some place.

'Despite all the advertising, there are a considerable number of us still in the Commonwealth. What are you doing?'

'Getting down to basics, my love.'

'But I can't see without my glasses. And I want to see!'

'You'll be closer to me than you've ever been to anyone before,' he promised. 'And you'll see.'

He picked her up again, carried her over to the bed, and tossed her on to it. The springs were new; she bounced, and gave a little squeal. Tighe, disgusted by the turmoil, walked over to the door and whined.

'You'd better believe it,' Charlie said as he opened the door and pushed Tighe out, then closed it behind him. The dog sat for a moment in the hall, whining, then gave up and waddled down the stairs.

Charlie Wheeler came back to the bed. 'Now, then, Miss Muffet,' he growled. 'I have you at my mercy.'

'C'mon,' she replied. 'No melodrama. This is serious business!' She squirmed. Just hearing his voice was sending thrills up her spine. Her mind was full of thoughts that ordinarily she would never entertain. Impatience had overcome modesty.

'When you're right you're right,' he agreed as he dropped on to the bed beside her. One of his hands rested imperiously on her breast, and she was finding it hard to breathe.

'We'll start from the bottom up,' he said and reached down to slip off one of her shoes. Just his touch on my foot, Leonie Wheeler told herself, is enough to light my fire! The future looks very bright indeed!

Tighe came waddling down the stairs, his grey nose snuffling. The pair of them were still standing there, looking upwards. 'What are they going to do now?' Cecilia asked anxiously.

'It's part of the new marriage system,' her aunt Agnes explained. 'They're going up to their room to debate the failure of the potato crop in Ireland.' She put the champagne bottle back into the refrigerator. Surely they'll have to come back down some time—soon? she thought.

'Failed potatoes? That's very important?' the little girl asked.

'Very.'

'Well, I can't spare them any more time. I have to watch *Star Trek* on TV. Wanna come and join me?'

'Why not?' Aunt Agnes said, sighing. 'We have to keep our priorities in order.'

HARLEQUIN ROMANCE®

brings you

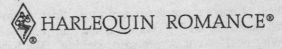

More Romances Celebrating Love, Families and Children!

We have a wonderful book for you in April in
our **Kids & Kisses** series—**Bachelor's Family,**
Harlequin Romance #3356, by the ever-popular
Jessica Steele. Fabienne Preston and Vere Tolladine
seem intent on misunderstanding each other until the
two adorable seven-year-old twins, Kitty and John,
play their part in the unfolding romance and make
their dream of being together a reality!

and coming in May...

Harlequin Romance #3362
The Baby Business
by Rebecca Winters

KIDS11-R

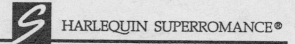

HARLEQUIN SUPERROMANCE®

**He's sexy, he's single...and he's a father!
Can any woman resist?**

First Love, Second Chance
By Amanda Clark

Julia Marshall is leaving New York City and going back to the Pennsylvania town where she grew up—even if there's not much to go back for. She'd been raised by cold, unloving foster parents. And she'd been betrayed by *Tommy Black,* the love of her teenage years. He'd promised to wait for her, to marry her, to love her forever. And he hadn't....

Now, ten years later, Tommy's a family man—with a family of two, consisting of him and his five-year-old daughter, Charlotte, better known as Chipper. When Julia comes back to town, Tommy discovers that he'd like nothing better than to make that a family of three....

Watch for *First Love, Second Chance* in April.
Available wherever Harlequin books are sold.

FM-3

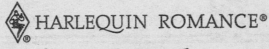

HARLEQUIN ROMANCE®

brings you

When you read **Invitation to Love** by Leigh Michaels, you will know there are some wonderful reading hours ahead of you with our **SEALED WITH A KISS** titles!

In April we have chosen **Dearest Love,** by Betty Neels, Harlequin Romance #3355, all about sensible Arabelle Lorimer and the rich and handsome Dr. Titus Tavener, who both seem to be agreed on one thing—that they make a very suitable couple. But what happens when love unexpectedly enters the picture?

Look out for the next two titles:

Harlequin Romance #3361
Mail Order Bridegroom
by Day Leclaire in May

Harlequin Romance #3366
P.S. I Love You
by Valerie Parv in June

SWAK-2R